Pay Cheques & Picket Lines

ALL
ABOUT
UNIONS
IN
CANADA

written by Claire Mackay

illustrations by Eric Parker

Kids Can Press Ltd.

Toronto

Kids Can Press Ltd. gratefully acknowledges the assistance
of the Canada Council and the Ontario Arts Council in the
production of this book.

331.884

Canadian Cataloguing in Publication Data

Mackay, Claire, 1930-
     Pay Cheques & Picket Lines

Includes index.
ISBN 0-921103-32-8 (bound) ISBN 0-921103-34-4 (pbk.)

1. Trade unions — Canada — Juvenile literature.
2. Trade-unions – Juvenile literature. I. Title.

HD6524.M24 1987   331.88'0971   C87-093181-4

1. Labour Unions —
2. Labour Unions
3. Goodwin,
4. One Big Union.
5. Winnipeg General Strik
6.

87   0 9 8 7 6 5 4 3 2

Book Design by Michael Solomon
Edited by Charis Wahl
Typeset by Alphabets Typesetting
Printed in Canada by union labour

Contents

Canada

Albert "Ginger".

e

TO THE MEMORY OF MY UNCLE,
BILL ARLAND,
MINER, SAILOR,
AND
GOOD UNION MAN

ACKNOWLEDGEMENTS

Without the help of many people, *Pay Cheques & Picket Lines* wouldn't exist. There isn't space to name them all, but to all of them I'm grateful, especially to:

Valerie Hussey and Ricky Englander of Kids Can Press, who came up with the idea; Wynne Millar, friend, fellow writer, and fine photographer; United Steelworkers' Libby Lee for buttons, contracts, information and sympathy, Monica Hewitt for photos, and librarian Jennifer Sells; Shirley Scarrow, OPSEU, for buttons and insights on shift work; Brenda Bolton, London Labour Council, for buttons and information about London unions in 1910; Joan McGrath, for her certainty that the book would be written, and her daughter Leslie, for buttons; Barrie Zwicker, writer and publisher, for buttons; Alison Pirot of Regina, Maggie Pym of Vancouver, and Susan Yates of Nanaimo, who got photos in a hurry; Clyde East, International Typographical Union, and Les Bronson, former reporter for *The London Free Press*, who went to extraordinary lengths; Jean Robertson, United Food and Commercial Workers, for the contract upon which Section 3 is based, and for her advice and encouragement; Wendy Cuthbertson, Canadian Auto Workers; Gordon Minns, International Brotherhood of Electrical Workers; Margaret Collier, ACTRA; Margaret Edgar, TV Ontario; Gordon Milling, who rekindled my interest in the labour movement; Pat Hancock, for sharing her memories; Bill Beach, who was on the picket line in the 1945 Ford strike; most of the unions in Canada, which gave me everything I asked for; the Canadian Federation of Labour, the Confederation of Canadian Unions, and the Canadian Labour Congress, for photos, articles, pamphlets, song and cartoon books, and several kilograms of other useful stuff; Michael Solomon and Eric Parker, whose design and illustrations have enhanced the text; Val Wyatt for her wise decisions and good humour; and the three people who were always there when I needed them—my mother, Bernice Bacchus, who typed hundreds of letters and made scores of phone calls; my husband, Jack, who for two years endured my single-mindedness and a house full of papers and books; and my editor, Charis Wahl, who did her magic trick again and made *Pay Cheques & Picket Lines* a better book.

INTRODUCTION

Most people are workers. Your parents, your teacher, your doctor, your school crossing guard, your bus driver, your favourite rock star or baseball player—all are workers.

Most workers work for somebody else: they have a boss. They work for the government of your country or province or city or town; they work for a school, a hospital, a small business like the pizza place on the corner or the T-shirt store in the mall, or a big business like Eaton's or General Motors or McDonald's. They work in a daycare centre or a disco, a furniture factory or a fish farm, a tennis court or a traffic court, a movie theatre or a morgue, an office or an orchestra, a radio station or a gas station, a cop shop or a pop shop. They hand you bus tickets, Blue Jays tickets, lottery tickets, Springsteen tickets, and speeding tickets. They make things, fix things, teach things, sell things, play things, clean things, haul things, write things, dump things, guard things, serve things, sing things, drive things, deliver things, build things, and wreck things.

And nearly half of them are union members. Out of every ten workers, four carry a union card.

What is a union? Why did unions begin? How did they grow? What do they do? Will they still be around when you start work?

Pay Cheques & Picket Lines answers these questions.

What is a union?

A union is a group of workers who join together to make their working lives better.

Unions aren't always called unions. Sometimes they're called associations, or federations, or guilds, or brotherhoods (even when women belong to them), or societies, or alliances, or leagues, or simply workers:

These people are all union members.

Canadian Airline Pilots Association
Quebec Federation of Hairdressing Employees
Canadian Merchant Service Guild
International Brotherhood of Painters
Manitoba Teachers' Society
Alliance of Canadian Cinema, Television and Radio
    Artists
Pattern Makers' League of North America
Food and Service Workers of Canada

Unions are different sizes. The biggest union in Canada is the Canadian Union of Public Employees (CUPE, pronounced "kewpie"). It has more than 300 000 members.

Margot Kidder

Gordon Korman

6

WHAT'S IN AN ACRONYM?

Unions are often known by their initials, and their initials often make acronyms, which look like words. Here's a list from the past and from the present:

CAME: Canadian Association of Mechanical Engineers

CAR: Canadian Artists' Representation

CAW: Canadian Automobile Workers

CUBE: Canadian Union of Bank Employees

CUTE: Canadian Union of Transportation Employees

FLU: Federal Labour Union

IAM: International Association of Machinists

NAME: National Association of Marine Engineers

NAPE: Newfoundland Association of Public Employees

ORC: Order of Railroad Conductors

PACT: Provincial Association of Catholic Teachers

PANS: Police Association of Nova Scotia

PIPS: Professional Institute of the Public Service of Canada

SONG: Southern Ontario Newspaper Guild

SUN: Saskatchewan Union of Nurses

And then there's IAMSSPRSTMSHMMTWH, which does not make a word, except perhaps in a distant galaxy. It's the union with the longest name: the International Association of Marble, Slate and Stone Polishers, Rubbers and Sawyers, Tile and Marble Setters' Helpers and Marble, Mosaic and Terrazzo Workers' Helpers.

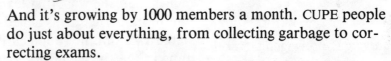

And it's growing by 1000 members a month. CUPE people do just about everything, from collecting garbage to correcting exams.

The smallest union in Canada is the International Association of Siderographers. It has four members. Siderographers do only one thing (but they do it perfectly!)—they make engravings on steel.

Unions are in different places. Radio station CKVU's Employees' Association is in one building. The Fort McMurray Independent Oil Workers is in one city. The Miramichi Trades and Labour Union is in one region. The United Nurses of Alberta is in one province. The National Union of Provincial Government Employees is in eight provinces. The Letter Carriers Union of Canada is in one country. The International Brotherhood of Teamsters, Chauffeurs, Warehousemen and Helpers of America is in two countries.

WHY DID UNIONS START?

Unions started because workers needed them. Here's why.

The street lamps still burned, throwing Mary's shadow first ahead, then behind her as she trudged through the soot-blackened snow. Icy water seeped through the cracks in her high, laced boots, and her feet grew numb. Ten blocks away, the City Hall clock boomed six slow beats, dignified as a funeral. Mary started to run. "I can't be late again," she whispered. She'd already lost half a day's pay—ten cents—for being late this week. Slush flew up with every step, drenching her skirt and shawl, but she paid no attention. Out of breath, soaked, and scared, she reached her place in the biscuit factory as the last hoot of the whistle echoed into silence.

The cookies kept coming, thousand after thousand, still hot from the huge ovens, never an end to them, dumped by the tray boys on the packing table in front of her. She gathered them in, ten at a time, with her left hand, while her right plucked a cardboard box from a tower of boxes, higher than she was, that leaned crookedly beside her. By mid-morning her arms ached with strain and her fingers were raw from the rough cardboard. Flour and biscuit dust hung in the air like mist, clogging her nose and throat. Her tongue felt like thick wool and she could barely swallow. She raised her hand for permission to get a drink of water. The foreman frowned, then nodded. "But you be sharp about it, girl!"

She clattered down the wooden stairs to the basement, remembering to leap over the space where two steps had rotted away. Last summer her friend Jennie had fallen there and broken her leg, and now she'd be lame all her life. Mary plunged the dipper into the old bucket, stained with rust where the handles had once been, and drank in huge gulps, her eyes blinking in relief.

The foreman threw her an angry look when she got back

A carriage and wagon factory posted the following Rules for Employees in 1872: "Employees shall daily sweep floors, fill lamps, clean chimneys, whittle pen nibs ... take one night a week off for courting, and if they are thrifty, faithful, faultless, attentive to religious duties, and stay out of jail, they will be given an increase of five cents a day after five years. That is, if profits justify it."

to her table. The pile of cookies was more like a mountain now, and she hurried to catch up. The cookies kept coming. Would they never stop? Would the noon whistle never blow? She had just decided it must be broken when it shrilled through the cave-like building.

Half an hour later it shrilled again. Mary jerked awake, her heart pounding in panic. She had eaten her bread and beef drippings in a patch of sunlight near the big dough mixers, then drifted into a doze. For a moment she wasn't sure where she was, and the foreman's shout seemed to come from far away.

"Back to work! Back to work! Rush orders for Christmas! Overtime tonight!"

Then he was standing over her. "On your feet, girl!" She looked up in time to see his hand swinging towards her. She tried to scramble out of the way, but the slap caught her hard, knocking her to the floor. Her teeth gouged her bottom lip, and the coppery taste of blood filled her mouth.

All through the afternoon, hour after hour, Mary packed cookies. Supper time came and went. Hunger raged in her, then faded, leaving her weak and sick. Her arms and hands moved mechanically, as if they didn't belong to her. The mountain of cookies shrank, grew, shrank, and grew again. One tower of boxes followed another and then another. She kept working.

The ache in her arms became a searing soreness. Her lip throbbed where the flesh had split. She kept working. Even after the whistle sounded, she kept working. Until a tray boy nudged her to stop. She stared stupidly at him, then wrapped her shawl about her and stumbled out into the cold and empty dark.

The street lamps burned, throwing Mary's shadow first ahead, then behind her, as she trudged through the soot-blackened snow. The City Hall clock struck ten. She'd soon be home, home from her job at the biscuit factory. Until tomorrow.

A hundred years ago, children didn't go to school very often or for very long, unless their parents were rich. They might get as far as grade three, or "third book," learning how to add and subtract, how to read simple things, and how to sign their names. After that, most of them left school and got jobs to help support their families. They worked in mines or mills or factories, ten or twelve hours a day, for as little as twenty-five cents.

Factory kids were often punished, sometimes just for talking to their friends while they worked. They were fined, or whipped, or locked in a small, dark, airless cellar room, called "the black hole," all alone, for hours at a time. Canadian author Bill Freeman describes a black hole in his novel *Trouble at Lachine Mill*:

> The darkness was like a smothering blanket that hung over Jamie's face. The black void pressed in on him from all sides. Fear began to build in his chest and for a moment he thought he would scream. His hands were trembling; his stomach was as tight as a knot.... He had to get out!...[Then] he heard...scurrying somewhere in the corner of his black dungeon. At first he didn't understand what it was. Then there was another rustling by his feet and a stirring by the door... Rats!

Boys as young as seven worked on the streets, selling papers or shining shoes. Many begged. Some stole. (And went to jail: one eight-year-old boy was sentenced to four years for stealing cigars.) A few pennies could buy a loaf of bread, or a piece of cheese, or a half-dozen potatoes, the three main foods of the poor.

Girls no more than eight years old worked at home taking care of their younger brothers and sisters. In those days, just like today in many families, both the mother and father had to work to make enough money to buy food and pay the rent. Sometimes, if the family had no money at all, or if a parent was sick, children were sent to orphanages for

a week or a month or a year, until the family crisis was past.

Some girls were sent to other peoples' homes, often far away from their parents, to be servants. They were given their meals, a bed to sleep in, and sometimes a penny or two—and for that they worked all day, nearly every day. Remember, there were no vacuum cleaners, no washing machines, and no Easy-Off oven cleaner. It took hours just to clean the stove—to scrape off the grease, gather the ashes, black the surface, and polish the pipes. And this was done every day.

Here is what one girl wrote to a Toronto newspaper in 1886:

> [A mistress] considers the servant a piece of machinery....The kitchen is...partly underground and poorly lighted, where the servant lives for the twenty-four hours....Where no other servant is employed, she is very lonely....The mistress, once or twice a day, visits to give orders. If a kind-hearted woman, she may give the girl a kind word, compliment her on her neatly ironed clothes, the clean floor, a bright stove. The servant's daily task ended, she can sit in this kitchen alone (alone also all day) or go to her own room, perchance a cold one at that, and when she gets tired of it [go to bed]. What is such a life but slavery!

Because each girl was alone in a household, it was hard to start a union. Another young woman wrote to the newspaper: "There is no association more needed than for servant girls. So many wrongs could be righted ... a general aim [should be] elevation of the despised, poor, isolated, degraded servant."

No matter what your job, it was dangerous. There were no safety rules, no protective clothing or goggles or hard hats, no safeguards on machinery. Thousands of working men, women, and children lost their health, their limbs, their eyes, and too often their lives. Here's a true story of one of those children:

My name is John Gale. I'm seventeen, and I haven't had steady work for five years now. Nobody wants to hire on a fellow like me, who's missing his right arm. I'm a hard worker, too. Leastways I was. I had a good job over in the sawmill on the bay. My dad got me in there before I was eleven, and I was making twenty-five cents a day. I worked at the circular saw, the two-footer, taking away the rough ends of the planks as they got trimmed. To this day I'm not sure what happened, but my arm got caught in the big cog-wheel that drives the machines and chewed it up like it was a sausage. I fainted dead away, right there in the sawdust. It happened just after the noon dinner whistle, but we had a good boss and I got paid for the whole day. Anyhow, I'm not as bad off as some. It wasn't two months later that another boy at the mill got both his arms and his legs taken off.

Many children were worked to death. Records from the United States tell us that, of every one hundred children with jobs, about thirty-five were hurt at work and four were killed. But we will never know how many died of illness caused by overwork, hunger, or dangerous substances in the work place.

Coal mining was like playing Russian roulette. In the mines of Nova Scotia, more than sixteen hundred men and boys died in seventy years. In British Columbia the numbers were worse: twelve hundred died in forty years, and no one is sure how many were hurt. In a book called *Boss Whistle*, two miners remember a mine explosion near Nanaimo, in which thirty-two died: "I went out to the mine to see them bringing out all the dead people. 'Course you couldn't see some of 'em, 'cause they was all burnt black you know. Yeh, the men was all burnt, killed in the explosion. And the mules and everything."

"I would be about five years old. I remember going into the big hall ... and the coffins — I can still see in my head the coffins stretched out in the hall."

Sometimes the whole family — grandparents, parents, and children — worked at home, sewing for clothing shops or department stores such as Eaton's.

They had to buy their own thread and their own sewing machines and needles. They had to walk to the factory or shop to pick up the cloth, and they had to deliver the finished garments. Often they worked from four in the morning till eleven at night. They did "piece work," which means they weren't paid by the hour or by the day or by the week, but were paid a certain sum of money for each garment, or for each job on a garment. For example, for cutting out, sewing, lining, and pressing

- a man's jacket: 26¢
- an overcoat: 37¢
- a vest: 17¢

For sewing buttonholes, workers were paid fifty cents a hundred.

The sweat shop is still alive and well in Canada: as you read this, more than 100 000 home-workers, most of them newly immigrated women with no union and no laws to protect them, are bent over their sewing machines. One of these women sewed the jeans you're wearing right now. She got one dollar for her work.

If they made mistakes they had to do their work over again, without pay. Many earned less than three dollars a week, and often the children worked for nothing.

This was called the "sweating" system. Sweated labour was just that: you worked long hours in terrible conditions, and you sweated for every penny you earned.

The places where this work was done were called "sweat shops." At first this meant a room in the house where the family members sewed, as you see in the photograph; but later it also meant a factory or store where many workers gathered to sew.

In the nineteenth century, working people had few laws to protect them. Wages were low. Hours of work were long. You could be fired for any reason or for no reason. If business was slow, you were laid off. Your pay stopped. Too sick to work? Too bad. Your pay stopped. Hurt on the job? Tough luck. Your pay stopped. Too old to work? No pay; no pension either.

Most people accepted this. They thought it was just the natural order of things, or fate, or the will of God. Some people were rich. Some people were poor. If you were born poor, you'd be poor all your life, and you'd die poor. So you worked as long and as hard as you could, took the pay the boss gave you, and figured you were lucky to get it. If you ever got a raise, you were really lucky.

A few dozen people had most of the money and all of the power. Tens of thousands of people had barely enough money to eat every day — and no power at all.

Workers started to think this was unfair.

Then they started to get angry.

Then they started to talk about what they could do.

Then they started unions.

How did unions grow?

Unions have been around longer than most people think. They started long before Canada did.

The first organized workers' groups in Canada appeared more than three hundred years ago. In 1657, Jean Levasseur, a master carpenter in Quebec City, founded a *confrérie*, or "brotherhood," a kind of club for carpenters and other workers. The members of the club helped one another in times of accident, sickness, and poverty, and together they opposed "injustices and shameful dishonesties." Other *confréries* followed. These clubs are the ancestors of today's unions.

Some of the injustices and dishonesties the confréries opposed were the treatment and wages of labourers sent from France. If they made it across the ocean alive — and a third of them didn't — they were paid at most ten dollars a year, and often nothing at all.

BY THE 1850s

When your great-great-great-grandparents were your age, Canada wasn't even Canada. It was called British North America. The population was about 2.5 million, which is less than the number of people who now live in Metropolitan Toronto. Most of them lived in the country. Farming was the most important occupation, and the whole family — parents and children — worked.

Cities were just beginning. Montreal was the largest city, with 90 000 people; St. John was the next largest, with about 55 000; and Toronto was third, with 44 000. But only nine places had more than 5000 inhabitants.

Industries were just beginning: shipbuilding and fishing in Newfoundland and the Atlantic region; logging along the Ottawa River; mills and foundries, small factories and businesses in Ontario and Quebec.

THE OLDEST UNION

One morning in 1832 a circular was handed out on the streets of Toronto:

"Owing to the many innovations which have been made upon the long established wages of the professors of the art of printing, and those of a kind highly detrimental to their interests, it was deemed expedient by the Journeymen Printers of York, that they should form themselves into a body, similar to societies in other parts of the world, in order to maintain that honorable station and respectability that belongs to the profession."

In other words, the printers started a union. Five years later, York was renamed Toronto and the union was renamed the Toronto Typographical Society. Now known as the Toronto Typographical Union, Local 91 of the International Typographical Union, it's 155 years old, the oldest union in North America.

Unions were beginning, too. Towards the end of this period, about five thousand people belonged to unions. All of them were men and most were highly skilled in a trade or "craft." (The word comes from an Old Norse word meaning "strength.") The unions they formed were called "craft unions."

Some of those crafts, and their unions, have vanished. New machines and new ways of doing work eliminated many jobs, as they do today. Here are a few of those vanished trades people:

- cordwainers: shoemakers. The word comes from the Spanish city of Cordoba, famous for its leather for more than nine hundred years.
- horologers: men who made clocks and watches. The Latin word "horus" means "hour."
- saddlers: men who made saddles and reins.
- carriage workers: men who built horse-drawn carriages.
- farriers: men who made horse shoes. From the Latin word "ferrum," which means "iron."
- riggers and sailmakers: men who made ships' ropes, spars, masts, and sails before the time of steamships.

If you look hard, you can still find a farrier, and maybe a saddler or two — but have you ever met a horologer?

Other crafts people — and their unions — are still very much alive. In 1850 there were:

- bakers, who belonged to the Bakers Friendly Association.
- carpenters, who belonged to the United and Friendly House Carpenters and Joiners Society.
- tailors, who belonged to the Benevolent Society of Tailors.
- printers, who belonged to the Society of Printers.

Nowadays ...

- bakers belong to the Bakery, Confectionery and Tobacco Workers International Union (16 000 members).
- carpenters belong to the United Brotherhood of Carpenters and Joiners (78 000 members).
- tailors belong to one of four different unions of garment and clothing workers, with a total of 50 000 members.
- printers belong to the Graphic Communications International Union (22 000 members) or the International Typographical Union (9600 members).

By 1850 there were around thirty-five unions, mostly of skilled craftsmen, in British North America. The unions were local — usually in one city or town — and the workers didn't know much and didn't care much about unions of their own craft in other places, or about unions of other crafts anywhere.

But the times were changing.

BY THE 1900s

When your great-grandparents were your age, the country had changed. It had a name: Canada. To the four provinces of Nova Scotia, New Brunswick, Quebec and Ontario, three more were added. Manitoba, half the size of New Brunswick and called "the postage-stamp province," joined Canada in 1870. British Columbia, bribed by the promise of a transcontinental railway, joined in 1871. Prince Edward Island joined in 1873, one year before Lucy Maud Montgomery, the author of *Anne of Green Gables*, was born. Canada stretched from sea to sea.

The people had changed. Half a million people came to Canada from almost every country in Europe between 1861 and 1870. Nearly 25 000 Chinese and Japanese came to British Columbia during the 1880s and 1890s, to work on the railways and in the mines and fish canneries. By the end of the century, Canada's population was nearly 5 400 000. More than a third of them — 1 890 000 — lived in cities. Old cities grew bigger, and new cities began.

Work had changed. Factories and mills sprang up everywhere; mass production of goods began. Railways, roads, and canals were built to transport the goods. Shops to sell the goods to the public began to appear. Sales clerks to serve that public were hired. Offices and office workers were needed to do the paperwork of all those factories, mills, mines, and shops.

"Company towns" were built near major resources, like coal or iron or lumber. The company that mined the coal or logged the trees also owned the town, including all the houses, the stores, and even the water supply. Workers got food and other necessities at the company store, and the cost of these items was deducted from their pay. Too often they finished a month's work to find out that nothing was left of their pay. Some of them owed money to the company all their lives.

In 1869, a young man named Timothy Eaton opened a small store in downtown Toronto. He hired two sales clerks to help him. By 1872 the store was doing so well he enlarged it and hired a dozen more clerks. These clerks worked in the mail order office. By 1987 his great-grandson, Fredrik Eaton, ran a huge department-store empire, with branches in every major city and a work force of thirty thousand.

There were still many thousands of highly skilled craftsmen, but the number of semi-skilled or unskilled workers employed by large companies, with little say about their jobs, was growing fast.

Knights of Labor organized two assemblies composed entirely of female shoemakers.

Unions changed, too.

Unions in the same craft or industry got together to form councils.

Unions in the same city got together to form trade assemblies.

Unions of miners in British Columbia formed the Miners' Mutual Protective Society in 1877.

Unions of miners in Nova Scotia formed the Provincial Workmen's Association in 1879.

Unions all across the country got together in 1886 to form a national labour organization, a sort of union of unions. It was called the Trades and Labour Congress of Canada, and it is a revered ancestor of the present Canadian Labour Congress.

American unions and groups of unions, such as the Noble Order of the Knights of Labor, came to Canada to organize Canadian workers. Quebec workers, badly paid and badly treated, flocked to the new American unions, and by 1900 there were 136 Quebec unions — up from 22 in 1880 — with 12 000 members, including a Muff Makers Union and an Electric Pole Climbers Union. The Catholic Church wanted Quebec workers to be in church-led unions. It didn't like the "outsiders," and it managed to get rid of them in the Great Shoemakers Lock-out (see p. 97).

"AND NEVER THE TWAIN SHALL MEET"

The Knights of Labor had a burning desire to organize everybody in sight, skilled and unskilled, men and women — but no Asians. Like most union members of the time, the Knights were opposed to immigrant workers. This was because the Chinese and Japanese people brought over by the railroad and the mining companies were paid far less than Canadian workers who did similar jobs. The Knights were afraid that employers would prefer to hire Asians, which would mean fewer jobs and lower wages for everybody else. Such anti-immigrant feeling has often appeared in Canada, usually in times of high unemployment.

Knights of Labor parade in Hamilton, where the first assembly was established.

KNIGHTS OF LABOUR PROCESSION
KING STREET HAMILTON

There was some heavy organizing going on, and soon after the turn of the century there were seventy thousand union members in Canada, fourteen times more than there had been fifty years earlier. Unions had spread beyond the skilled artisans to include garment workers, hotel and restaurant employees, metalworkers, miners, loggers, telegraphers, and just about everybody who worked on the railroads, including the drivers and conductors and stable hands (who looked after the horses that pulled the carriages) of the city street-railway companies.

As the new century began, unions had more strength, more respect, and a greater sense of common purpose.

But the times were changing.

BY THE 1950s

About the time your parents were born, Canada had changed still more.

It had a tenth province, Newfoundland, and two territories, the Yukon and the Northwest.

It had fought two terrible wars.

It had survived the Great Depression of the 1930s, when one in four people were out of work.

Its population grew to more than fourteen million, partly because of the "baby boom" after World War Two — in 1960, one-third of the people were younger than fourteen — and partly because hundreds of thousands of immigrants came to Canada from all over the world.

Cities were bigger, and farms were still disappearing. By 1956, two out of every three people lived in cities.

Dozens of inventions and new processes appeared, among them the radio, hydroelectric power, plastic, the airplane, television, the transistor, and, most important of all, the car.

New ways of doing work were developed: the assembly line, machines that built machines, automation.

Women went out to work in great numbers, especially during the two world wars. And many of them wanted to keep working, even after the wars were over. This meant changes, too, both for industry and unions.

High schools (secondary schools) were invented. So was adolescence. Young people no longer left school after grade six or eight to get a job. During the Depression you couldn't get one anyway.

Unions multiplied during these years.

Each invention meant whole new industries; each new industry meant new workers; new workers meant new or bigger unions. (The opposite happened, too. The car meant the end of the Carriage Workers, the Saddlers, and the Harness Makers unions. Diesel oil meant the end of loco-motive firemen, who tended the coal fires in steam engines.)

In 1913, Henry Ford had a bright idea: as if he were slicing a loaf of bread, he neatly divided a mechanic into thirty-seven parts and rigged up a belt that moved. Presto! The assembly line. It was great for Henry, but not so great for the worker, who now did only one tiny job over and over again all day, every day. He was as interchangeable as a bolt.

A Model A Ford rolled off the assembly line every three minutes.

Canadian poet Dorothy Livesay wrote about the assembly line in a long poem about work entitled "Day and Night." Here is the first stanza:

> Dawn, red and angry, whistles loud and sends
> A geysered shaft of steam searching the air.
> Scream after scream announces that the churn
> Of life must move, the giant arm command.
> Men in a stream, a human moving belt
> Move into sockets, every one a bolt.
> The fun begins, a humming whirring drum —
> Men do a dance in time to the machines.
> One step forward
> Two steps back.

An early meat-packing assembly line.

25

There were two main groups of union workers — and they didn't like each other much. The craft unions banded together in the old Trades and Labour Congress (TLC) and in 1902 joined the U.S. craft union organization, the American Federation of Labor (AFL), which was international. Then the AFL kicked out the Knights of Labor, who vanished around 1910, and any union that competed with an AFL union for members. The unions that had been expelled got together with the new industrial unions and the railway unions, and in 1927 formed the All-Canadian Congress of Labour (ACCL). By 1940 the ACCL had gathered in tens of thousands of new members from the mushrooming mass-production industries. It linked up with the lively young Congress of Industrial Organizations (CIO) in the United States, and dropped the first word from its name —

Not all unions belonged to the TLC or the CCL. Some of those that didn't scared the wits out of governments and employers. They had revolutionary ideas about how society should be run, how work should be organized, and — most alarming of all — how wealth should be divided. Many people agreed with them. After World War I, in which 60 661 young Canadians were slaughtered — equal to the entire population of Lethbridge — and after the Depression and a terrible drought that made almost everyone else poor, ordinary people felt bewildered, betrayed, and angry.

Here are a few of those revolutionary groups:
- Mine workers: In the West and the East, and in northern Ontario, independent mineworkers' unions sprang up and waged many long and violent strikes. Only one of these unions is still around: the Mine, Mill and Smelter Workers, at Falconbridge nickel mine in Ontario.
- The Wobblies: Founded in 1905 in Chicago, the IWW (Industrial Workers of the World, called "Wobblies") spread into mining, logging, and railway camps of the western provinces. They believed that all workers should belong to

one union, and that workers should own and run the mines, mills, factories, and shops.
- One Big Union: The OBU grew out of the IWW and played a large part in the Winnipeg General Strike of 1919.
- Workers' Unity League: The WUL was part of the Canadian Communist Party. Begun in 1929, it soon had unions among miners, loggers, and garment workers, and in many industries that had never had a union.

it was now the Canadian Congress of Labour (CCL). In Quebec, Catholic unions and a number of Canadian unions formed the Canadian Catholic Confederation of Labour (CCCL) in 1921. By 1930 seventy-two thousand workers — one in ten — were union members. During the rule of Maurice Duplessis (1936-1939 and 1946-1959), called the "Great Darkness," unions were persecuted and oppressed. After World War Two, violent strikes in the cotton, asbestos, and copper industries began to weaken the church's hold on Quebec's unions.

The labour movement began this period by splitting apart and ended it by getting together again. In between there was plenty of action. And violence.

Strikes were frequent, major, and often dangerous. Property was stolen, damaged, wrecked, blown up, or torched. People taking part in strikes were clubbed, beaten, kidnapped, stoned, tear-gassed, deported, jailed, shot, or drowned.

Unions spent a lot of time fighting. Sometimes the bad guys were the bosses, sometimes the government, sometimes the police (local, provincial, or the Mounties), sometimes the army, sometimes hired muscle men and strike-breakers, sometimes other unions. And sometimes all of them at once.

Now, fifty or sixty years later, it's hard for us to understand how some of these things happened. Why were people beaten or killed or jailed or banished from Canada just for belonging to a union? Why did police fight strikers? After all, police officers of today have unions of their own. It doesn't seem right, or fair, or even possible.

The answer, or part of it, is that during those years governments and employers were frightened by the new ideas about power, work, and money held by many Canadians, especially those who belonged to unions. They were even more frightened when the Depression came along in 1930, and hundreds of thousands of jobless, homeless,

Why were IWW members called "Wobblies"? According to H.L. Mencken's huge book The American Language, it happened this way: In 1911, an immigrant restaurant owner in Vancouver who was just learning English gave free meals to customers carrying the small red union membership card with the initials IWW. He pronounced them "Eye, Wobble, Wobble." IWW members were delighted with him — and the meals — so they called themselves "Wobblies."

A regiment of riflemen was sent to Steveston, B.C. during a 1900 strike. The army showed up at all major strikes until the mid-1930s, and occasionally after that. In 1941, four hundred soldiers were sent to Arvida, Quebec, during a strike by aluminium workers; and the army was called to "keep order" in the Montreal police and fire-fighters' strike of 1969.

hungry, angry men and boys roamed the country. Some government leaders thought Canada was on the brink of revolution, so at the first sign of protest — on a picket line, at a picnic, in a private house, or in a public hall — they sent in the police or the army.

They also passed laws that we would find harsh today. People who spoke out against the government or suggested different ways to share the country's wealth were seen as suspicious, even dangerous, and could be arrested. The Communist Party was outlawed and all its leaders were put in jail. Union organizers and ordinary union members, especially those who went on strike, were often called "Communists" and were put in jail, too. If they hadn't been born in Canada, they were called "foreign agents," or "dangerous aliens," and were forced to return to the country of their birth, leaving behind their wives and children. This happened to ten thousand people between 1931 and 1934. For a while there was even a law that said no language other than English could be used at public meetings. It was a tough time to belong to a union.

But out of the turmoil and suffering and struggle came growth. In 1956, the Trades and Labour Congress and the Canadian Congress of Labour finally stopped fighting and merged, to become the Canadian Labour Congress (CLC). More than a million workers carried a union card, twenty times the number at the turn of the century. Most of them came from the new mass-production industries, whose growth was spurred by World War II: steel, aluminum, chemicals, automobiles and trucks, aircraft, communications, synthetic rubber, plastics, and food processing.

Some of them — not many, but some — worked in offices and stores; some belonged to professions such as engineering and teaching and nursing; and some were employed by city, provincial, or national governments. It was a sign of the future: white-collar workers were joining unions.

The times were changing.

Ever since we peeled the hides from woolly mammoths and put them on our own, we've used our clothes to tell people who we are or where we live or what we do for a living. Sometimes the clue is an item of clothing; sometimes it's a colour; sometimes it's both. These special clothes or colours may come to stand for the people who wear them. For example, a British soldier, whose uniform coat was red, was called a "redcoat."

In the labour movement, the colour of your collar was the clue to the work you did. With the arrival of the T-shirt and the turtle-neck, collar colours don't mean as much, but the words themselves are still used, and useful, to describe certain kinds of workers.

A *blue-collar* worker was originally someone who wore blue or dark-coloured clothes to his job as a labourer, miner, longshoreman, or someone who did hard manual work. Blue-denim jeans, overalls, and shirts were worn as early as 1850. They didn't show dirt, sweat, or wear as much as other clothes. Now a blue-collar worker is anyone who works with his or her hands.

A *white-collar* worker is someone who works in an office. The phrase was first used in the 1920s, when more and more people had jobs as clerks and bookkeepers and secretaries. These workers wore stiff white collars, which were detachable: they were fastened to the shirt with buttons, and were removed at night to be washed and starched for the next day.

A *pink-collar* worker is a woman who has a low-paying, dead-end office, sales, or service job. The phrase was first used in the mid-1970s, in a book entitled *The Pink Collar Ghetto*. Pink is regarded as a "feminine" — and rather unimportant — colour.

A *steel-collar* worker is a robot. The phrase, which appeared in 1985, is sometimes used as a joke, and sometimes used in anger.

A *new-collar* worker is the son or daughter of a blue-collar worker, with a higher-paying job than his or her parents.

Here are some other workers named for the clothes they wear:

- brass hat: a high-ranking officer in the armed forces, because of the gold or brass-coloured decorations on the cap; a big boss
- redcap: a porter who carries your luggage at the train station
- skycap: a porter who carries your luggage at the airport
- blackrobe: a priest; a missionary in early Canada
- bluecoats, or blues: uniformed police officers
- green hornet: Toronto city worker who gives out parking tickets, "green" because of the colour of the uniform and "hornet" because of the noise of the motorbike
- gumshoe: a detective, who wears shoes with gum-rubber soles in order to be stealthy
- saboteur: a person who wrecks machines or equipment. The first saboteurs were silk weavers in Lyons, France. In 1801 their boss, Joseph Jacquard, invented the automatic loom, and installed several of them in his factory. The weavers thought they might lose their jobs, so they burned the looms and destroyed the factory. At that time most French workers wore *sabots*, or wooden shoes.

29

The Victims

The list of deaths was long, for both sides.

▲ Ginger Goodwin, a fiery organizer for the mineworkers in British Columbia during World War I, was found unfit for military service because of tuberculosis. Later, in 1917, he took part in a smelter strike in Trail, and was ordered to join the army. He refused, and as he was running away he was shot by military police. British Columbia workers staged a one-day general strike in his memory on August 2, 1918.

Viljo Rosvall and John Voutilainen, organizers for the Lumber Workers' International Union and experienced outdoorsmen, vanished near Onion Lake, in northwestern Ontario, in November 1929. Neither the police nor the Ministry of Lands and Forests would search for them, and union search parties were barred from the area. Their bodies, terribly mutilated, were found in April 1930. The photograph of Rosvall is dated 1927. ▼

Monument to Nick Nargan, Pete Markunas, and Julian Gryshko, coal miners from Bienfait, Saskatchewan, who were shot during a parade of strikers and their families on September 29, 1931. Many others were wounded, and were turned away from the nearby hospital in Estevan because they couldn't pay for a week's care in advance. When it was first erected, the stone read "Murdered in Estevan September 29, 1931 by the RCMP." The last two words have been chiselled away. A poem about this tragedy was written in 1932, and was later set to music. It's one of the few original Canadian labour songs. ►

▲ Monument to René Fortier, Fernand Drouin, and Joseph Fortier, lumber workers on strike against Spruce Falls Power and Paper Company, who were ambushed by strike-breakers at Reesor's Siding, near Kirkland Lake, Ontario, on February 10, 1963. Eight others were wounded. The killers were later fined $100 for carrying offensive weapons. The union was fined $27,600 for "unlawful assembly."

Vancouver, British Columbia, 1903: Frank Rogers, vice-president of the Fishermen's Union, murdered by thugs said to be working for the CPR, for supporting the railway workers' strike.

Oakalla Prison, British Columbia, 1914: Joseph Mairs, twenty-one years old, sentenced to eighteen months of hard labour for "unlawful assembly" during a mine strike, died of tuberculosis.

New Waterford, Nova Scotia, June 11, 1925: William Davis was shot by special police hired by the British Empire Steel Company during a protest to get water service restored. The water supply, owned by the company, had been cut off in an attempt to end a strike.

Wayne, Alberta, Christmas Day, 1928: James Rafferty, a striking coal miner, was bludgeoned to death by a company watchman.

Regina, July 1, 1935: The On-to-Ottawa trek of the unemployed was stopped in Regina. During the riot that followed, Detective Sergeant Charles Millar, in plain clothes, was beaten to death.

Blubber Bay, British Columbia, 1937: After a brutal strike the vice-president of an International Woodworkers of America local was arrested and beaten so badly he later died. The constable who beat him got six months in jail.

Badger, Newfoundland, March 11, 1959: Police constable William Moss died of injuries after a clash with striking loggers, whose union, the International Woodworkers of America, had been declared illegal by Newfoundland Premier Joey Smallwood.

TODAY

Canada is still changing. There are more of us: twenty-six million in 1987. There are more kinds of us. Since 1950, close to four million men, women, and children have moved to Canada. They've come from Europe, especially Italy, Greece, and Portugal; from Africa and India and Pakistan; from the islands of the Caribbean; from Central and South America; from Korea and Vietnam and China and the Philippines. Perhaps your parents were among them.

Most of these new Canadians settled in the cities, adding to the people who had come earlier from farms and small towns. Now four out of five Canadians live in cities, and only one in twenty works on a farm.

Ordinary life has changed. More of the people have more of the money. Although Canada still has many poor people, most families have running water, electricity, a radio, and a television set. The number of cars on the road has jumped from four million in the late 1950s to sixteen million, and the number of telephones from five million to seventeen million.

It's been a time of marvels: moon landings, heart transplants, Velcro, rock videos — and the silicon chip. This tiny device, the brain of the computer, altered our lives forever.

Work has changed. Only three out of ten workers now actually make things, produce goods you can touch. The other seven do things. They work in what is called "the service sector": governments or schools or banks or stores or restaurants or sports or television studios or cruise ships or symphony orchestras.

Millions of these service workers are women. Nearly half the people who go to work are women. After World War II, the number of women taking jobs grew enormously. It was partly because of the new feminism — women wanting to do work other than, or as well as, housework and being mothers — and partly because the women needed money. Inflation — when a dollar buys less and less — had hit the

HELLO HELLO HELLO HELLO HELLO HELLO
On our seventeen million telephones we make twenty-seven billion calls a year, a world record. That's about eleven hundred calls for every Canadian man, woman, child, and teenager.

country, and soon most families needed the wages of two people.

It almost seems as if life hasn't changed for working people in a hundred years, but this isn't true. In the 1880s everyone in the family had to work to make enough money just for food, fuel, and rent. In the 1980s, children don't work, and all of us expect and want a bit more than our great-great-grandparents had: a holiday, or a movie now and then, or a new pair of runners, or a T-bone steak. These are simple, ordinary things, but they're beyond the budget of many families, unless both parents bring home a pay cheque.

The three largest unions in Canada are public-service unions:

- Canadian Union of Public Employees (CUPE) — 305 000 members
- National Union of Provincial Government Employees (NUPGE) — 255 000 members
- Public Service Alliance of Canada (PSAC) — 182 000 members
- And the ninth-largest union in Canada is a teachers' union, the Quebec Teaching Congress (Centrale de l'enseignement du Québec), which has 86 000 members.

Unions changed and grew, too. There are now nearly 3 800 000 people in Canada who belong to eight hundred unions.

In Quebec, almost half the workers belong to unions. After Maurice Duplessis died in 1959, Quebec was changed forever by a series of educational, social, and language laws, which together were called "The Quiet Revolution." The leaders of this revolution were teachers and public servants, eager to join old unions or start new ones. After a slow start and a persecuted history, unions in Quebec are strong, and laws covering workers are the best on the continent.

Three of every ten Canadian union members — 1 200 000 — are women. Many of those women have become leaders in their locals and of their unions. And in 1986 a woman took over the leadership of the "union of unions": Shirley Carr was elected president of the Canadian Labour Congress.

Women have made their employers and their unions think about new ideas: maternity leave, paternity leave, equal pay for work of equal value, and daycare centres in the work place. Some of these ideas have become reality. And women have helped to foster a new awareness in the labour movement of issues beyond the work place: poverty and oppression in other countries, the health of the environment, and the peace of the world.

But most of the new union members come from a part of the labour force that had never before been unionized — the public service: letter carriers, tax accountants, secretaries, game wardens, garbage collectors, librarians, forest rangers, sewer workers, nuclear engineers, weather forecasters, road-repair crews, police officers, fire-fighters, meat inspectors, hospital cleaners, and playground supervisors — all the people who work for you and me and are paid by governments.

Madeleine Parent: Born to wealthy parents and educated in private schools, at age 20 Madeleine Parent decided to devote her life to helping workers, especially women. A tireless and courageous union leader from 1940 to the present, Ms. Parent was a key figure in the 1946 MOCO strike (see page 74), and in many strikes since. In 1969 she and her husband Kent Rowley founded the Confederation of Canadian Unions (CCU).

Shirley Carr: The first woman president of the Canadian Labour Congress is a coal-miner's daughter who left school at 16. In 1960 Ms. Carr was elected to the executive of Local 133 of the Canadian Union of Public Employees (CUPE) in Niagara Falls. She rose to become general vice-president of CUPE. In May 1986 she was chosen to lead the CLC, the biggest congress of unions in Canada.

Grace Hartman: Nicknamed "Amazing Grace," Ms. Hartman began work at age 16 to help support three younger sisters. Her union career started in 1954 when she worked as a typist in North York, Ontario. She was leader of her local in 1959, and came up through the ranks of CUPE to be its president in 1975, the first woman ever to lead a major Canadian union. In 1981 she went to jail for leading Ontario hospital workers in an illegal strike. She retired in 1983.

Despite the figures, the past thirty years have not been easy for unions. They have been challenged by world-wide depressions; permanent unemployment for hundreds of thousands of young people; layoffs of many thousands of workers in mining and metal-making, car and airplane manufacturing, foods and clothing; competition from low-wage Third World countries; new technology; and new laws, especially in Alberta and British Columbia, that endanger workers' rights. The times are changing.

Everybody has a Union

Athletes have unions:
- The National Hockey League Players' Association, with 154 Canadian members and seven Canadian teams
- The Major League Baseball Players' Association, with eighty Canadian members and two teams (the Toronto Blue Jays and the Montreal Expos). Association members have been on strike four times since 1972
- The Major League Umpires Association, who went on strike during the 1984 World Series
- The Ontario Harness Horsemen's Association, who boycotted the racetrack in 1985

Writers have unions:
- The Writers' Union of Canada (TWUC), who boycotted Classic Bookshops and W.H. Smith book stores in 1986, to support sales clerks trying to get their first contract
- League of Canadian Poets
- Industrial Writers' Union, whose members write about work
- Playwrights Union of Canada (PUC)
- Periodical Writers Association of Canada (PWAC)

- Freelance Editors' Association of Canada (FEAC)
- Writers Guild, Alliance of Canadian Cinema, Television and Radio Artists
- Union des écrivains québécois
- The Newspaper Guild

Musicians have unions:
- American Federation of Musicians (AFM), who don't like the disc jockeys because they often get hired instead of live musicians
- Disc Jockeys Association, who aren't crazy about AFM members because they often get hired instead of disc jockeys
- Recording Musicians' Association
- Composers, Authors and Publishers Association of Canada

Actors, painters, cartoonists, clowns, comics, puppeteers, announcers, photographers, film editors, magicians, impressionists, dancers, mimes, camera persons, sculptors, quiz-show hosts, video artists, set designers, and movie makers have unions:
- Canadian Artists Representation (CAR)
- Canadian Actors Equity Association
- Canadian Association of Editorial Cartoonists
- Independent Artists Union
- Performers Guild, part of the Association of Canadian Cinema, Television and Radio Artists
- American Guild of Variety Artists
- Union des artistes
- American Federation of Radio and Television Artists
- The Directors' Guild of Canada
- International Association of Theatrical and Stage Employees
- National Association of Broadcasting Employees and Technicians

Even people who aren't working have unions:
- Unions of unemployed workers, active in London, Toronto, and elsewhere. Such unions have always sprung up during depressions in Canada; for example, in the 1870s, the 1930s — and the 1980s. Recently, jobless tradesmen in Alberta formed a union called the Dandelions, who pester the government to do something about the unemployment rate. They chose the name "dandelion" because, as one member said, "You can poison it and stomp on it, but you can't get rid of it." Politicians have found mysterious crops of paper dandelions on their lawns.
- Students' unions, in most colleges and universities. They discuss college rules, food services, and other matters with the administration. Student unions aren't in elementary schools yet. But you could always start one.
- The Kids' Union of Canada (KUC), started by a Calgary boy in 1985, takes part in peace parades, protest marches, boycotts, and other labour demonstrations.

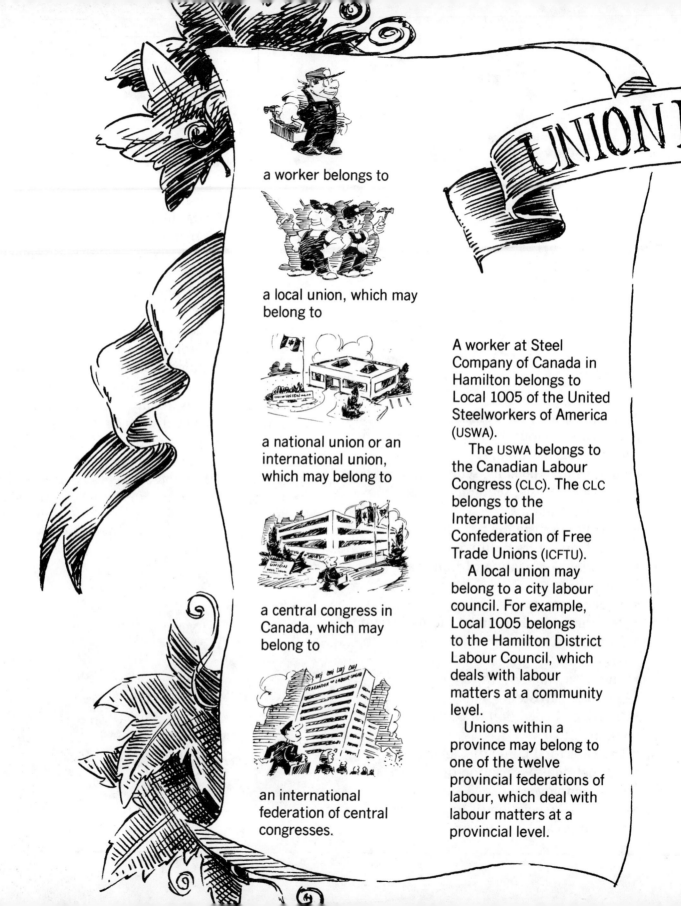

a worker belongs to

a local union, which may belong to

a national union or an international union, which may belong to

a central congress in Canada, which may belong to

an international federation of central congresses.

A worker at Steel Company of Canada in Hamilton belongs to Local 1005 of the United Steelworkers of America (USWA).

The USWA belongs to the Canadian Labour Congress (CLC). The CLC belongs to the International Confederation of Free Trade Unions (ICFTU).

A local union may belong to a city labour council. For example, Local 1005 belongs to the Hamilton District Labour Council, which deals with labour matters at a community level.

Unions within a province may belong to one of the twelve provincial federations of labour, which deal with labour matters at a provincial level.

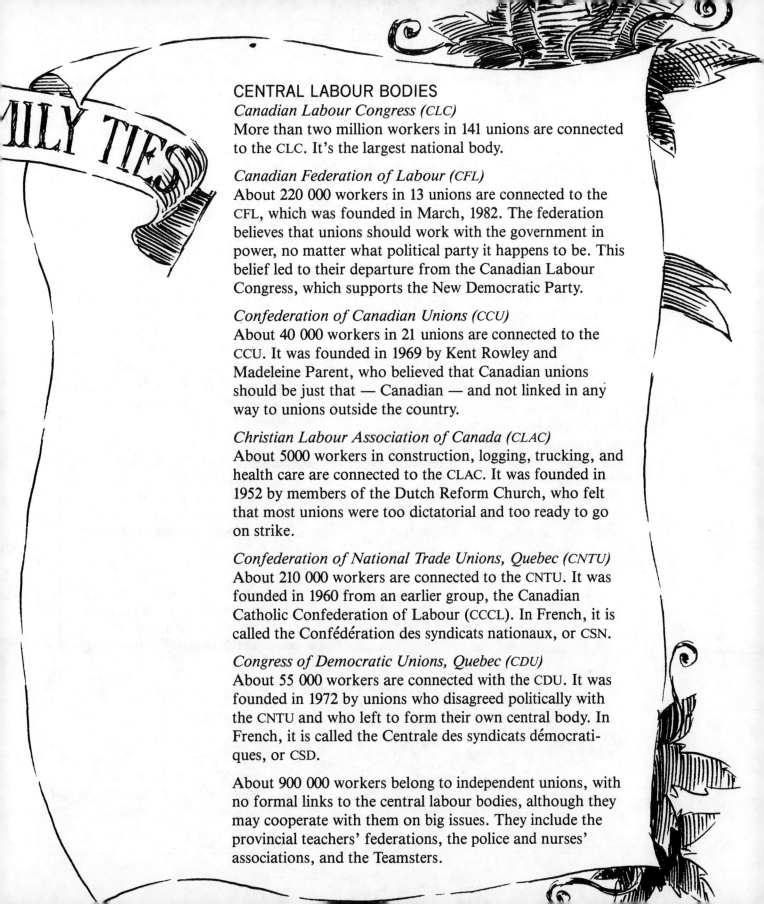

CENTRAL LABOUR BODIES

Canadian Labour Congress (CLC)

More than two million workers in 141 unions are connected to the CLC. It's the largest national body.

Canadian Federation of Labour (CFL)

About 220 000 workers in 13 unions are connected to the CFL, which was founded in March, 1982. The federation believes that unions should work with the government in power, no matter what political party it happens to be. This belief led to their departure from the Canadian Labour Congress, which supports the New Democratic Party.

Confederation of Canadian Unions (CCU)

About 40 000 workers in 21 unions are connected to the CCU. It was founded in 1969 by Kent Rowley and Madeleine Parent, who believed that Canadian unions should be just that — Canadian — and not linked in any way to unions outside the country.

Christian Labour Association of Canada (CLAC)

About 5000 workers in construction, logging, trucking, and health care are connected to the CLAC. It was founded in 1952 by members of the Dutch Reform Church, who felt that most unions were too dictatorial and too ready to go on strike.

Confederation of National Trade Unions, Quebec (CNTU)

About 210 000 workers are connected to the CNTU. It was founded in 1960 from an earlier group, the Canadian Catholic Confederation of Labour (CCCL). In French, it is called the Confédération des syndicats nationaux, or CSN.

Congress of Democratic Unions, Quebec (CDU)

About 55 000 workers are connected with the CDU. It was founded in 1972 by unions who disagreed politically with the CNTU and who left to form their own central body. In French, it is called the Centrale des syndicats démocratiques, or CSD.

About 900 000 workers belong to independent unions, with no formal links to the central labour bodies, although they may cooperate with them on big issues. They include the provincial teachers' federations, the police and nurses' associations, and the Teamsters.

THE WORLD OF WORKERS

Working people of all countries have always felt close to one another. They share the same hopes — for steady jobs, fair wages, and good working conditions — and they fight the same battles to realize those hopes. Out of that sense of unity, of solidarity, came the Wobblies (Industrial Workers of the World) in the early 1900s, and three later international associations of unions.

• World Confederation of Labour: The WCL, founded in The Netherlands in 1920, has eighty member groups, mostly Catholic and Protestant labour federations, from seventy countries. It represents fifteen million workers. The Canadian member is the Quebec Confederation of National Trade Unions (CNTU).

• World Federation of Trade Unions: The WFTU was founded in 1945, and at that time it was truly global in membership. In 1949 most of the large labour federations in the western world left it to form the ICFTU. Now the WFTU has fifty-five members, mostly in eastern Europe and the USSR but also including Italy and France, and it represents 140 million workers.

• International Confederation of Free Trade Unions: Founded in 1949 after a split with the WFTU for political reasons, the ICFTU has 136 central labour congresses as members, and it represents eighty-five million workers in ninety-five countries. The Canadian member is the Canadian Labour Congress.

At its founding, the ICFTU issued what is now called the Bread, Peace and Freedom Manifesto. This is what it says:

BREAD
The task before us is to mobilize the tools of abundance possessed by the industrially advanced nations of the world to ensure full employment, security against want, old age and sickness, and to provide ever-rising standards of living and a richer and fuller life for peoples everywhere.

PEACE
A movement of free and democratic peoples — united in a common effort to achieve economic security, social justice, and political freedom — is the only basis on which lasting peace can be established.

FREEDOM
Unite with us to achieve a world in which people are free from the tyranny of totalitarianism, as well as from the domination and exploitation of concentrated economic power in the hands of cartels and monopolies.

What do unions do?

You just landed a job as a dishwasher in Piggin' Out, the restaurant over in the mall.

Piggin' Out has class. It's got tables. On the tables are white tablecloths. On the tablecloths are glass vases. In the vases are real flowers. Fresh every day. Class.

But you soon find out it's not such a great place to work. The job is hard. You have to work nights whenever the boss says so. What with sweeping the floor and cleaning the sinks, sometimes you don't get out of there until two in the morning, even though your shift — and your pay — stops at midnight. You don't get paid for the extra time, and when you're only making four dollars an hour, every penny counts.

What's more, the manager goes into orbit if you drop a dish; the hostess, known as the Dragon Lady, gives the tables near the washrooms — where the customers never tip — to any waitress who talks back to her; Mark the busboy has been waiting three years for a promotion; and last week the assistant chef just about went up in flames because the fire extinguisher doesn't work.

Everybody grumbles a lot. But not out loud. If you complain, you don't have the job long.

One night it's really busy. The customers keep coming and so do the dirty dishes. Mark drops a trayful of glasses and the manager freaks out. One waitress is crying, another is swearing, and another is plotting to barbecue the Dragon Lady and serve her on a bun with French fries. Free. Then Brenda, who always gets the tables near the washrooms, says, "What we need around here is a union!"

And everybody else says, "Right on, Brenda!"
Now what?

Getting Organized

After the restaurant closes that night, you invite the whole gang back to your place for a meeting. You don't ask the manager or the Dragon Lady: they are your bosses, and bosses aren't allowed, by law, to be in the same *bargaining unit* as the people they boss. So you, Mark, the chef, the assistant chef, the cashier, and Brenda and the other waitresses sit around, drink pop, and try to decide what union to join. You might want to be completely on your own, in which case you'd be the Piggin' Out Workers (POW). But usually it's a better idea to join — to become a *local* of — a larger national or international union. The big unions have experienced people who can help you get a good contract, and often provide strike pay if you need it. You go for the big one, and decide to join the Glorious Order of Restaurant People (GORP). Then, since it's three o'clock in the morning, everybody goes home to bed.

The sign-up

On your way to work the next day, you drop in at GORP headquarters and get some membership applications. You hand them out on your coffee break or when the Dragon Lady isn't looking. Most of the gang sign up on the spot and give you a couple of dollars for the initiation fee, which is required by law.

Certification

Since more than half the workers — a majority — signed up, you take the applications to the Ministry of Labour in your province and ask to be *certified*. Certification is very important: it means you get a certificate — a legal paper — that says the Piggin' Out owners must bargain with your union only. They can't make a private deal with any other union, or any other group, or any other person. If the application forms are filled out properly — and if the Piggin' Out owners don't try to stop you — you are granted certification.

HOW EMPLOYERS TRY TO KEEP UNIONS OUT

Many companies don't want their employees to belong to a union. To prevent it, they might use a carrot:

They pay such good wages that the employees are just as well off as if they belonged to a union. (If there weren't any unions, of course, employers wouldn't have to pay good wages. In this way, unions help raise wages in non-union companies.)

Or they might use a stick:

They get rid of the workers who want a union by (a) firing them; (b) moving them to other locations; or (c) reclassifying them as supervisors or managers, who aren't allowed to be in a union, and then firing them. Such tactics are against the law, but they are still sometimes used by management.

Even after a company has a union, there are ways to get rid of it. Big corporations, with more than one branch, sometimes close the unionized branch. Sometimes they move (in which case they are called runaways) to a place — often in another country — where wages are low and unions are weak or don't exist.

EQUAL PAY FOR WORK OF EQUAL VALUE

Should a telephone operator be paid as much as a parking-lot attendant? Should a nurse earn the same as a computer analyst? Should a grocery clerk's wages equal those of a delivery person?

Since 1978, when the federal government passed a law requiring equal pay for work of equal value for the businesses it controls — following the lead of Australia, Britain, much of Europe, and thirty-one American states — business, labour, governments, and women's groups have been talking about it. Quebec, Manitoba, and Ontario now have similar laws, which may soon cover public servants, teachers, and hospital workers. Women are particularly concerned, because their wages have always been much less than men's, even when they did work requiring equal or greater skill.

It isn't as simple as equal pay for equal work, which means that two workers doing the same job should receive the same pay. It involves measuring the value of a job, based on skill, effort, responsibility, and working conditions.

Many employers think it will cost too much money, and they are against it. But as one woman remarked, "They were against the abolition of slavery, too."

All systems are now go: The Piggin' Out gang is GORP Local 007, and is entitled to bargain with the Piggin' Out owners to get a *collective agreement* or *contract*.

Then all the members of Local 007 have a meeting to elect an *executive*, the members of the local who will conduct the business of the local. Brenda is elected president; you're elected shop steward. This is an important position: you are the link between the workers and the employer if *grievances* (complaints) arise. Then you decide what you want in the contract, and pick a *negotiating team*. The team will have three or four members, who will do the talking when you meet the bosses. You and Brenda and Mark are picked. Then the team has a meeting with the bosses of Piggin' Out to try to reach an agreement about wages and working conditions. This is called *collective bargaining*. It may take days or weeks or months, but finally you have a contract.

Then all the members of Local 007 have another meeting to *ratify* the contract; that is, they vote to accept what's in it.

The Contract

You just got a copy of the contract. It looks good: it's fifty pages long, typed, and signed by Brenda and the manager. On the front it says: COLLECTIVE AGREEMENT between PIGGIN' OUT LIMITED and LOCAL 007 GLORIOUS ORDER OF RESTAURANT PEOPLE, January 1, 1988 – December 31, 1989

Wages

The first thing you want to know is how much money you'll make. You turn to the page headed "Wage Schedule." And you smile. Each job at the restaurant, and the pay per hour for each job, is listed.

And there you are: dishwasher. You're now making $5.25 an hour. Decent! And in a year you'll be making $5.75.

JOB	1st year	2nd year
Cook	$6.65	7.35
Assistant Cook	6.05	6.75
Cashier	5.75	6.35
Dishwasher	5.25	5.75
Busperson	4.50	5.00
Waitress/Waiter	3.85	4.25

WAGE SCHEDULE

According to <u>The Guinness Book of World Records</u>, the longest work week ever is 142 hours, worked by an English doctor in 1980. Which left him three hours, forty-two minutes and fifty-one seconds a day to eat, sleep, watch TV, and hang out.

SHARING THE WORK

All the provinces and territories have laws setting hours of work per week. Five have a forty-hour limit, the others forty-four to forty-eight. Many unions want limits on overtime and a forty-hour week nationwide, so that more people can have jobs. In Ontario, if all the workers who have jobs worked only forty hours a week, half of the unemployed — 200 000 people — would have full-time jobs.

PROTECTOR OF THE PIGS

Why are you called a shop steward?

To find out, we have to visit a farm in England 1500 years ago. Let's look at the cows first. They're in a "<u>scipen</u>" (cowshed). This word, pronounced "shippen," changed over the years to "<u>schoppe</u>," which meant a stall or a booth, not only for cows, but for other farm products sold in the town market. From "<u>schoppe</u>" it was an easy jump to "shop," a place where things are sold, or where things are made to be sold later, or where work is done. We still have workshops, machine shops, body shops, barber shops, and cop shops.

Now let's look at the pigs. There, tending the pigs, we find a "<u>stigweard</u>." "<u>Stig</u>" meant "sty," a pen for the pigs; and "weard" meant "warden," a watchman or protector. "<u>Stig</u>" later came to mean a hall, or a house, or any building in which property was kept or where people lived and worked. And the <u>stigweard</u> looked after that property and helped to run the business of the house or building. Gradually the spelling changed to "steward," and the meaning broadened to include the modern trade-union meaning, guardian of the work place.

So your job as shop steward is to make sure the rules of your work place — as agreed to in the contract — are not broken, and that the rights of the workers are secure.

Hours of work

You wash dishes. But you also ski, swim, play Dungeons and Dragons, sing in a choir, and collect comic books. You need money and time to do these things. You're ready to work for the money, but how much time will it take to earn it? The contract spells it out:

> "The standard work week for full-time employees shall consist of forty hours per week comprised of five eight-hour days."

Overtime

Next you remember how you didn't get paid for those extra hours after midnight, cleaning the sinks and sweeping the floor. You find the section in the contract called *Overtime*.

> "Overtime at the rate of time-and-a-half (1½) the employee's regular rate shall be paid for all work performed:
>   (a) after eight hours in a day;
>   (b) after forty hours in a work week."

Now, if you work past your regular hours, you not only get paid, but you get paid at one and a half times your usual rate, or time-and-a-half. So if you work two hours extra, you get paid as if you worked three hours. Instead of making zip, you'll make $15.75.

Shift premium

Then you remember what a drag it is to work the night shift, and you read the section called "Shift Premium" to make yourself feel better:

> "A shift premium of fourteen cents an hour shall be paid for any afternoon shift (2:00 P.M. to 10:00 P.M.) or night shift (4:00 P.M. to 12:00 midnight)."

Now you get fourteen cents an hour more than your usual pay, or $5.39 an hour, when you have to work nights. Not much, but better than nothing.

SHAFTED BY SHIFTS

Many workers hate shift work. It wrecks family and social life. Because it disturbs sleeping and eating patterns, it can even make you sick. Doctors call it "Rotational Shift Syndrome Disease." The shift from midnight to 8:00 A.M. is least liked. Back in 1915, somebody called it the "graveyard shift," and the phrase stuck. It refers to the lonely hours of night when ghosts may lurk in the cemetery — or when you feel like a zombie.

Your great-great-grandfather probably worked twelve hours a day, six days a week, a seventy-two-hour week. Now most work weeks are forty hours or less. But it wasn't easy getting from there to here. In 1872 the nine-hour day, six days a week, was a hot issue, with parades, rallies, fierce arguments, and strikes. Hamilton printers won their strike for shorter hours and were remembered in verse:

THE BIG YAWN
There are sixty million shift workers in the world. Because their sleeping-waking cycle is upset, each year they lose seven thousand years of sleep.

THE NINE-HOUR PIONEERS
by Alec Wingfield

Honor the men of Hamilton,
The Nine-Hour Pioneers;
Their memory will be kept green,
Throughout the coming years.

And every honest son of toil
That lives in freedom's light
Shall bless that glorious day in May
When might gave way to right.

Your cause was just, your motives pure,
Again, again, again,
You strove to smooth the path of toil
And help your fellowmen.

And Canada will bless your name
Through all the coming years,
And place upon the scroll of fame
The Nine-Hour Pioneers.

SANTA CLAUSES

Some contracts have special clauses that give workers more money.

- reporting time: If you show up for work and there's no work to do, you get paid for half a shift, or four hours, even though you just turn around and go home again.
- double time: When you work on a holiday, like Christmas or Labour Day, you get twice your usual pay for that day, or double time.
- danger pay: For dangerous jobs — building skyscrapers or digging oil wells in the ocean or taking the temperature of fresh lava — you get extra money.
- isolation pay: If your job is in a remote place that doesn't have supermarkets or discos or parking meters or telephones or people — perhaps weighing the snow on Baffin Island — you get extra money.
- COLA: This doesn't mean you get a free Coke. It means that your wage rate will go up if the inflation rate goes up. That is, if it starts costing you more to buy food and pay the rent, you will get extra money, a Cost of Living Adjustment (COLA).

016016

Fringe Benefits

Brenda is happy about this part of the contract. Last year she broke her foot while hang gliding and missed six weeks of work. She missed six weeks of pay, too. It'll never happen again, and not just because she's given up hang-gliding and taken up cross-country skate-boarding. Now Piggin' Out workers have paid sick leave, which means they get full pay for up to two months, depending on how long they've worked. This is a *fringe benefit*, and most contracts have many. They may include medical, dental, and drug plans, partly or totally paid for by the employer; pensions, partly or totally paid for by the employer; bereavement leave, usually three paid days off when a family member dies; and maternity and paternity leave, when a baby arrives.

Union Security

The money looks good. But will it last? What if the cashier or the cook drops out of the union? What if Piggin' Out starts hiring new people who won't join the union? What if there's no union left after a year? You see a section called "Union Security," and you stop worrying, because this is what it says:

> "All employees who are members of the union shall remain members of the union as long as they work at Piggin' Out; and all persons who become Piggin' Out employees shall join the union within a month of being hired."

This is called a *union shop*.

It looks as if Local 007 will always have members, but unions need money, too. It's part of union security. All employees — even in the first month of employment, before they become union members — pay dues, often an hour's pay per month. This is the law. The dues money goes to the union's headquarters. Some of it pays for the rent, electricity, and telephones, the office supplies and the printing of contracts, and the salaries of people who do research or help in bargaining with employers. And some of it may come back to you as strike pay, if Local 007 ever goes on strike.

Does this mean that you'll have to run around every month and collect dues? What if a member won't pay? What if a member punches you in the mouth instead? Then you read the next paragraph:

"Piggin' Out agrees to deduct the dues authorized by the union from the first pay of each month for each employee, and to give this money to the union by the middle of the month."

This is called the *checkoff*. It's in most Canadian contracts.

Time Off

Remember Bob Cratchit in *A Christmas Carol* having to ask Scrooge for a holiday on Christmas? That won't happen to you. The length and number of breaks and holidays are part of your contract. You get two fifteen-minute breaks, a half-hour for lunch, and nine holidays — New Year's Day, Good Friday, Victoria Day, Canada Day, Civic

---

Must all workers in the bargaining unit be union members? In Canada, there are four answers to this question.

1. Yes, even before they're hired. This is called a closed shop and it is found mainly in the craft unions. For example, a construction company that has a contract with the United Brotherhood of Carpenters and Joiners must hire carpenters who are UBCJ members. Similarly, doctors, lawyers, and engineers can't practise unless they join a professional association.

2. Yes, a certain time (usually a month) after they're hired. This is called a union shop, and most of the contracts in Canada — including yours at Piggin' Out — follow this pattern.

3. Yes, except for the workers who were there before the union was organized. This is called a modified union shop.

4. No, but all workers must pay union dues, since all are receiving benefits from the union. This is called an agency shop, or a Rand Formula shop.
(See page 73)

49

Holiday, Labour Day, Thanksgiving, Remembrance Day, and Christmas. You also get a "floater," an extra day off each year. Floaters are in many contracts, and workers often take them on their birthdays.

Vacations with pay weren't even thought of until the twentieth century. Now everybody gets them. The longer you work, the longer your vacation. At Piggin' Out, you get two weeks after working one year, three weeks after five years, four weeks after twelve years, and five weeks after twenty-five years.

Seniority

Mark the busboy likes this section. He wants to be an assistant cook, but twice in the past three years Piggin' Out has given newer employees the job. Now, because of seniority — the length of time a person works for the same company — he'll have his chance. A list is kept of how long each employee has worked. The employee with the longest service is at the top, and the employee with the shortest service is at the bottom. Promotions, the choice of vacation times and work shifts, and layoffs depend on how long you've worked. Sometimes you see the initials LIFO (Last In, First Out) or FILO (First In, Last Out). This means that, if business is bad and the company has to cut down its work force, the employee who was hired last will be the first to lose his job, and the employee who was hired first will be the last to lose his job. Seniority keeps things fair.

The grievance

A grievance is a complaint from a worker who believes that the employer hasn't lived up to the contract or has broken the rules of the contract. Every contract has a *grievance procedure*. Both employers and unions see it as very important: it can clear up small problems before they become big issues.

For example, Cindy, the cashier, gets the flu one afternoon, and goes to lie down in the employees' rest room. She still has three hours left in her shift, but she's too sick to work. Mark the busboy says he knows how to do cash and offers to take over. The Dragon Lady, who is leaving the next day for a new job as head of a prison camp in South America, says it's okay with her. So Mark finishes Cindy's shift.

When payday comes two weeks later, Mark looks at his cheque and gets mad. As a busboy, he earns $4.50 an hour. But the contract says that if an employee does another job at a higher rate for three hours or more, he gets paid for those hours at the higher rate. A cashier makes $5.75 an hour, so Mark thought he'd get an extra $3.75. He didn't. He decides to put in a grievance. And here's where you, as shop steward, do your thing.

Step 1 Mark explains his problem to you. Both of you then talk to the new hostess. She says she wasn't there when it happened, so she can't settle it. You must now go to Step 2.

Step 2 Mark fills out a grievance form and gives it to Piggin' Out's manager, Lucretia Macbeth. The next day Lucretia tells Mark that he's out of luck: a grievance must be filed within ten days of the event that caused it, and Mark didn't complain until two weeks later. Mark is now ready to smash all the dirty dishes. You calm him down, and go to Step 3.

Step 3 It's time for the big guns. You phone GORP headquarters and ask for help. They send over their best troubleshooter, Serena Pacifico. Lucretia Macbeth phones the head office of Piggin' Out. They send the vice-president of human resources, Clint Westwood. Serena and Clint go over the grievance. Clint starts shaking his head, but Serena says: "Hey, Clint, listen up. The grievance was caused by the pay cheque, not by Mark taking over as cashier, right?" Clint says: "Right." Serena says: "And Mark complained as soon as he got the cheque, right?" Clint says: "Right."

WANTED: PIED PIPER OF HAMILTON

In 1985, city workers in Hamilton filed a grievance about mice — both dead and alive — with which they shared the work place.

Serena says: "So Macbeth's out to lunch, and you owe Mark $3.75, right?" Clint says: "Right." End of grievance. Mark gets his money.

If Clint and Serena hadn't settled it, the grievance would go to Step 4.

Step 4   This is called *arbitration*. The grievance is settled either by an arbitrator, an outside person something like a judge or a referee in a hockey game, or by an arbitration board of three people, one picked by the employer, one picked by the union, and a third person, approved by both employer and union, who chairs the board. Whatever they decide is final. Arbitration is the last step. You can't take the grievance any further. Even if you don't like the decision, you can't go on strike.

Health and safety

The assistant cook — Brenda calls him the Human Torch — pushed hard for this section. Part of it says:

> "The Company shall keep in the restaurant four fire extinguishers, in proper working order, which shall be inspected at regular intervals and accessible to employees."

Piggin' Out must also supply first-aid kits; hair nets, so you won't get your hair caught in the meat grinder or the customers' food; beard nets, for the same reasons; rubber gloves for the dishwasher; safeguards on equipment and machines; and transportation to a hospital if necessary.

Accidents

One reason work can be dangerous is that accidents can happen. An accident happens in seconds. If you, as a dishwasher, slash your thumb with a carving knife or scald your arm when the water's too hot, that's an accident.

Let's look at some numbers.

THE PRICE OF PAIN

In the year 643 AD, Rothari, King of the Lombards, a people in northern Italy, ordered builders to make payments to their injured labourers. They did, but they didn't much like it, and after Rothari's death, compensation for a work injury vanished. For almost 1300 years, the general view was that if a person took a job, he or she had to take the risks of the job: it was the worker's fault if he or she got sick, hurt, or killed. In the twentieth century, partly because of union pressure, Rothari's idea reappeared. The first law in Canada for injured workers was the Workmen's Compensation Act of Ontario, passed on April 28, 1914. Since 1949, all provinces have had compensation laws. The money comes from employers, just as Rothari ordered thirteen centuries ago. They pay an amount, based on the accident rate in their industry, into a central fund. The province then pays this money to injured workers and their families.

• For every working day lost in Canada because of strikes and lock-outs, six are lost through accidents and disease.

• Two of the safest jobs are teaching school and working in a dynamite factory. In the factory, the workers are so scared they obey all the safety rules. Two of the most dangerous jobs are farming and digging tunnels. In 1984 and 1985, one hundred farmers died in Ontario alone, mostly from accidents with tractors and machinery.

• The job of being the Human Cannonball in a circus may shorten your body as well as your life. When seventeen-year-old Sue Evans was fired from a cannon in 1978, she was one centimetre shorter when she landed.

WORST INDUSTRIAL ACCIDENT IN HISTORY:

In December 1984, an explosion at the Union Carbide plant in Bhopal, India, released chemical fumes that so far have killed more than 2500 and injured or made sick half a million people.

WORST MINE ACCIDENT IN HISTORY:

In April 1942, a coal dust explosion killed 1572 miners at the Honkeiko colliery in China.

WORST NUCLEAR ACCIDENT IN HISTORY:

On April 26, 1986, an explosion at a nuclear power plant in Chernobyl, USSR, spread radioactive particles over a wide area. So far, thirty-one have died, but experts say extra cancer deaths in the next seventy years may reach two thousand. A sad side-effect was the destruction of the Laplanders' way of life: their reindeer are now the most contaminated animals in the world, with radiation levels thirty times higher than normal. Selling reindeer meat, which was how the Lapps made money, is now banned.

Each year, a thousand Canadians die and one million are injured in accidents on the job. Out of that million, twenty thousand are hurt so badly that they can never go back to work. This is one injury every six seconds, and one death every two hours of the working day. Accidents cost Canada billions of dollars yearly.

Most deaths are from falls, collisions, derailments, fires, explosions, gassing, and electrocution. Recently a new hazard has arisen: terrorist bombing of airports and planes. Pilots, flight attendants, clerks, mechanics, and baggage handlers — not to mention passengers — are worried. Unions of the workers involved are asking for tighter security, and in 1986 IFALPA (International Federation of Airline Pilots Associations) said it would boycott countries that harbour or encourage terrorists.

Occupational Disease

The other way work can be dangerous is by making you sick. Unlike an accident, a disease may not show up for weeks or months or years. If you, the dishwasher, develop a rash from the detergent or a cough from breathing the stuff you clean the garbage cans with, that's an occupational disease.

Let's look at some numbers.

Each year, more than ten thousand Canadians die and forty thousand are permanently disabled from occupational diseases. This means that, in each working day of a forty-hour, five-day work week, one worker dies every three minutes, and every twelve minutes a worker gets too sick ever to work again.

What do workers get sick from? Here's a short list:

Noise, dust, vibration, heat, cold, fumes, smoke, continuous repetitive movements, bad design of tools and equipment, radiation, chemicals, emotional stress, and boredom.

Mad as a hatter?

Some occupational diseases are part of our everyday speech:

- Mad as a hatter: Do you remember the Mad Hatter in the book Alice in Wonderland? Did you ever wonder why he was called that? In earlier times, mercury was used to stiffen the felt in hats. Long exposure to mercury destroys the nervous system and damages the brain.
- Punch drunk: This doesn't mean zonked from the great stuff in the punch bowl at your cousin's wedding. Every time a boxer gets punched in the head, little blood vessels in his brain break and bleed, reducing the flow of oxygen. After a while he may have trouble walking, talking, and thinking. He looks and acts drunk.
- Athlete's foot: A fungus infection between the toes.
- Tennis elbow: Inflammation of the tissues around the elbow joint. Carling Bassett isn't the only person who might get it: violinists, telephone operators, and clothes pressers can suffer from it, too.
- Housemaid's knee: Constant pressure on the knees while cleaning floors can cause a painful swelling, called "bursitis" by doctors.

Other diseases aren't as well-known — except to the people who have them:

- Chauffeur's fracture: Broken elbow, sometimes found in drivers who drive with their left elbow sticking out the car window. It happens when the elbow is hit by a bus, a tree, a brick wall, or anything harder than the driver's elbow.
- Diver's palsy: This is also called "the bends." Divers who rise to the surface too fast — moving from high pressure to low — suffer dizziness, pain, and tremors.

- Farmer's lung: Breathing problems caused by mouldy hay.
- Glass-blower's cataract: Eye injury from the intense heat used in making glass.
- Meat-packer's asthma: The plastic wrap used to package meats is cut by a hot wire. The melting wrap gives off fumes that cause shortness of breath.
- Welder's ague: One form of what's called "Monday fever." Workers in many industries often get fever symptoms on Monday that get worse during the week, go away on the weekend, and return the following Monday. It comes from breathing an irritating substance at work. With welders, it's zinc oxide fumes.

And you can also get:

- Black lung, or pneumoconiosis, common in miners of soft coal. The dust from the coal scars and hardens the lungs. Breathing becomes a struggle.
- Brown lung, or byssinosis, in textile workers exposed to cotton, flax, and hemp dust. The dust irritates the small air tubes in the lungs and they fill up with a thick brownish fluid. Bronchitis and emphysema may follow.
- White finger, or Raynaud's Disease, in miners, loggers, automobile sanders, jackhammer operators, or anyone using vibrating equipment. The blood vessels in the hands are damaged, and for a short time the finger or fingers are white and numb. The whole hand may be painful, movements are clumsy, and cold weather makes it worse. In bad cases, the fingers develop ulcers and gangrene.

Chemical killers

Industry uses fifteen thousand harmful chemicals, and a new one is invented every twenty minutes. We don't know yet how dangerous most of them are. We do know that two out of three work places contain cancer-causing substances. And we're now finding out that many jobs are especially dangerous for girls and women. Chemicals and radiation can alter cell structure and cause the workers' babies to be born dead or deformed.

Computer casualties

The office computer is blamed for headaches, vision problems, boredom, fatigue, and stress-related heart troubles. New evidence points to another frightening possibility: radiation from computer terminals may cause birth defects. But perhaps the most common disorder is "high-tech disease," or tenosynovitis, in which the muscles and the tissue covering arm tendons are inflamed. It's found in employees, mostly female, who work with business machines all day, pressing keys as often as ten thousand times an hour. It hurts — and it can cripple.

From the time they began, unions have fought to make work safe. The fight continues. Now every union has a health and safety department, every local has a health and safety committee, and every contract has a health and safety clause. That clause can be more important than any other: it may one day save your life.

Without unions, the list of dead and disabled workers would be far longer. Without unions, most of our laws and much of our knowledge about occupational health and safety would not exist. Without unions, the Canada Labour Code would not now say that every worker has:

- the right to know about dangers in the work place;
- the right to share in making the work place safer; and
- the right to refuse work that is unsafe.

THE ASBESTOS TIMEBOMB

Asbestos is a mineral made up of almost indestructible microscopic fibres, and it's a killer. Although its manufacture and use is now limited, it can still be found in more than three thousand products, including home insulation, brake linings, cement pipe, and children's toys. Doctors, scientists, insurance companies, and the asbestos industry knew of its dangers by 1920, but until a few years ago nobody told the workers who'd been breathing it.

Now tens of thousands of workers, their wives, and their children (the men brought the fibres home on their clothes) are slowly and painfully dying of asbestosis, which scars the lungs until they don't work; lung cancer; and mesothelioma, an incurable cancer caused only by asbestos. A quarter of a million North Americans will die from illnesses caused by asbestos by 2010. This is more people than were killed by both atomic bombs in World War II.

THE NO-NAME EPIDEMIC

Women making computer chips and integrated circuits in California's Silicon Valley are getting sick. There's no name for what they have, but the symptoms are frightening: loss of memory, depression, colds and infections, constant nausea and headaches, miscarriages, and trouble walking and concentrating. Doctors think that long exposure to the poisonous chemicals used in electronics manufacture has damaged their immune systems. This has led to a lower resistance to illness, and to what's called "chemical hypersensitivity." The women are now allergic to anything containing the chemicals they worked with — including perfume, hair spray, deodorant, oven cleaner, ink, paint, and wood stains. Since more than a million women work in the industry, the no-name disease may be an epidemic by 1990.

Contracts unions don't like

You and the rest of the Piggin' Out gang have a contract that gives you fair wages, good working conditions, and a say in what goes on at work. But there are contracts that do the opposite: workers are cheated of a decent wage, the work place has bad vibes, and nobody has the nerve to say much.

Yellow-dog contract

This is an agreement between an employer and a worker, usually arranged secretly before hiring or promotion, that the worker will not join a union. Once common, it is now illegal. A "yellow dog" is a mongrel, a dog of mixed breeds, and therefore not highly valued. (Mongrels' fur is often yellowish.) A "yellow dog" came to mean someone of weak character whose loyalty could be bought. The phrase entered American slang in the 1840s and spread rapidly after Abraham Lincoln used it in a speech around 1858. "Yellow-dog contract," with its special anti-union meaning, was a common phrase by the 1890s, and it's still with us.

Sweetheart contract

This is a contract arranged by a union leader for the members of the union, in which the leader accepts poorer terms in return for a secret payoff from the employer. The leader and the employer are said to be "sweethearts." Sweetheart contracts are rare, because in most unions the details of the contract must be made known to the members, who vote on whether to accept them. But what seemed to be a sweetheart contract made headlines in 1985,

CANADA'S SWEETHEART

This was the name given to Hal Banks, an American organizer for the Seafarers' International Union (SIU). Banks was a brutal thug who had been charged with assault twenty-seven times, served a jail term for manslaughter, and kicked a man to death.

In 1949, Banks was invited to Canada by the government, the shipping companies, and the Trades and Labour Congress to destroy the Canadian Seamen's Union (CSU), which was accused of being Communist. By 1951, using threats, fists, boots, baseball bats, bicycle chains, and guns, he had smashed the CSU and signed up most of Canada's sailors in the SIU. He arranged sweetheart contracts with all the companies with whose top brass he was on very friendly terms. The reign of terror came to an end in 1962, when at last the government could no longer ignore the violence. After an eight-month investigation, Banks was convicted of conspiracy to commit bodily harm and sentenced to five years in prison. He jumped bail and escaped to the United States, where he ran a profitable water-taxi business in California until his death — of natural causes — in 1985.

when evidence in a trial showed that the president of a union local was paid $250,000 by Consumers' Distributing Company. He didn't tell the tax folks in Ottawa about the extra money, and he was sent to jail for income tax evasion. The company was fined $125,000 for illegal kickbacks.

It's nearly two years later. Your contract is about to expire, so you and Brenda and Mark start meeting with the bosses to negotiate a new contract. After eight meetings, things are at a standstill. You want a raise of thirty-five cents an hour for everybody. They say they'll give you ten cents. You want an extra holiday. They want to cancel the floater. Negotiations stop. Meetings stop. There's only one way to go: Local 007 prepares for a strike.

The Strike

The first strike in Canada may have been as early as 1652. It was a tough year for the fur trade. The Iroquois were raiding the French forts and attacking the traders during portages. The supply of beaver pelts dwindled. The fur merchants ordered their *coureurs de bois* — the early name for voyageurs — to travel farther and paddle faster for the same pay. The men refused, saying life was too short. They were right: most of them were dead before they were thirty-five.

The life of a *coureur de bois* was adventurous and free, but it certainly wasn't easy. He carried loads of 68 kg (150 pounds) over tricky portages, some of which were 72 km (45 miles) long. One wrong step could bring death. His daily supply of food was sometimes only a few ounces of fish and a handful of corn. He slept in a blanket full of fleas. He had to put up with clouds of black flies and mosquitoes, and crowds of irritated Iroquois. Working conditions were not the best.

Although the *coureurs de bois* didn't have a contract like that of Local 007, they did have an agreement with the merchants about matters such as the distances travelled, the price per pelt, and rest stops during the longer portages. They felt the merchants had broken this agreement. They threw down their paddles and wouldn't pick them up again until the merchants backed off.

Nowadays, a strike occurs when the old contract has expired and the employer and workers can't agree on a new contract; or when the union has been certified but the employer refuses to bargain for a first contract. After a time set out by law, the workers can go on strike. A vote is held, and, if a majority of workers chooses a strike, the union executive orders the members to walk out. Picket lines — workers carrying signs informing the public that a strike is in progress — are set up around the work place. If the union can afford it, the strikers get strike pay for as long as the strike lasts.

The strike is the last resort. Nobody wants a strike, and nobody likes a strike, especially the strikers. Walking a picket line in rotten weather and getting strike pay — usually far less than your usual pay — is no fun. But if workers and employers can't agree on wages and working conditions, the only weapon workers have is to withhold the only thing they can sell: their labour. They strike. Without the right to strike, working people have no power at all.

Sometimes, when you read the paper or watch the news on TV, you might think that everybody, including the dog, is out on strike. That's because strikes make the headlines, just like wars and accidents and snowstorms and hijackings and floods and the birth of quintuplets. After all, you don't expect the newspaper to print a story that begins, "An accident didn't happen at the intersection of Hotrod Boulevard and Hospital Avenue on Saturday night." Can you imagine CBC radio starting the six o'clock news with: "No one is being held hostage at the Transylvanian Embassy this week"? You haven't seen a prime-time television show about how the weather's been quite nice lately. And you'll never read, hear, or see a news item that says, "Most of the world's workers went to work today."

Why? Because it's boring. There's nothing dramatic or exciting or shocking about the fact that ninety-five out of every hundred contracts are settled without a strike.

MOTHERS OF THE WORLD, GOOF OFF!
At the 1985 United Nations Conference on Women, delegates called for a world-wide one-day strike of all women who work in the home. If it ever happens, it will be the biggest strike in history, with about two billion people taking part. And six million Canadian kids will have to find their own socks.

Millions of workers have never walked off the job, and they wouldn't know a picket line from a clothes-line.

As long as records have been kept in Canada, there's never been a year in which the time lost through work stoppages — strikes by workers and lock-outs by employers — has reached one percent of the total time worked. Put in another way, of every hundred days worked by all workers in all of Canada, only six hours is missed because of a strike.

A strike can be simple and straightforward: you can't get a contract, you vote, and you walk out. But there are other kinds of strikes, other ways to protest, and other methods of sending a message to the employer and the public. Let's look at some of them.

Sit-down strike

The sit-down is exactly that: workers, especially assembly-line workers who must stand up to do their jobs, sit down and refuse to work.

In Canada, the first sit-down strike was at the Kelsey-Hayes Wheel Company in Windsor in 1936. The workers had formed Local 195 of the United Auto Workers (the first Canadian UAW local) and they wanted two things. First, they wanted union recognition, which means they wanted the company to accept the fact that Local 195 had the legal right to represent the workers. Second, they wanted the company to lower the number of wheels they had to make each day. The company said no. The workers sat down and stopped working. The strike was over minutes after club-swinging police arrived.

But the sit-down strike that captured headlines and scared the government took place at the Holmes Foundry in Sarnia in 1937. Conditions were terrible: men were choking in dust and collapsing from heat. There was no place to wash up or eat lunch. Shifts were nine hours long with one half-hour break a day. Many of the workers were European

UMPIRE OUT AFTER STRIKE CALL

The first recorded sit-down strike took place at a baseball game in Akron, Ohio. Two teams from the nearby rubber factories wouldn't play because the umpire didn't belong to their union or any union. The players sat down on the field until a union member was found to act as umpire.

The sit-down strike is the theme of a favourite union song, part of which goes like this:

When they smile and say,
"No raise in pay,"
Sit down, sit down;
When you want the boss to
come across,
Sit down, sit down.

Chorus:
Sit down, just take a seat,
Sit down, and rest your feet;
Sit down, you've got 'em
beat,
Sit down, sit down!

immigrants, and it was they who formed a union. The strike began on March 1 and ended in a brutal riot on March 3. Encouraged by the employers, the police, and the Ontario government, a mob of 325 men invaded the foundry, shouting insulting names. They were armed with clubs, pick handles, iron bars, and blackjacks. Twenty strikers were badly hurt; many were in hospital for months. The mob then swarmed into the strikers' tiny homes and stole or smashed their few belongings.

Hit-and-run strike

This is also called a rotating strike. Groups of workers in a factory, or in a company with many branches, take turns striking, usually without warning. The employer never knows which part of the operation will be hit, and the whole system stops. Postal workers and doctors have used this tactic.

Sympathy strike

This is a strike by workers not directly involved in a dispute, to show support for workers who are involved. It's against the law, and employers usually get a court order to stop it.

Wildcat strike

This is an illegal strike, in which workers walk off the job against the rules of the contract and against the wishes of their union. But it certainly gets the employer's attention.

Some workers can't strike. Some don't want to. They use other tactics.

Slow-down or go-slow

The slow-down is just what it says. Workers put less effort into their jobs so that production drops, often drastically. Sometimes the slow-down is in revenge for the speed-up, in which an employer orders the workers to work faster for the same hourly wage.

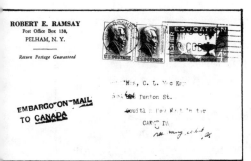

During a 1968 postal strike, all mail from the United States was stopped at the border.

Work-to-rule

This tactic has the same effect as a slow-down. Workers obey absolutely every law, rule, regulation, and procedure, no matter how silly, in connection with their jobs. Working-to-rule has been used with great success by psychiatrists, police, postal workers, bus drivers, government clerks, and teachers.

Mass resignations

In 1970, when the Board of Education refused to reduce class size, six thousand Metro Toronto secondary school teachers handed in their resignations. The Board changed its mind.

POSTIES CANCEL MAIL

In 1965, a wildcat postal strike, the first big work stoppage in the post office since 1924, was a turning point for Canadian unions. The clerks, sorters, and carriers, angry at low pay and hundreds of mean little rules, walked out. The strike spread all across Canada, and the workers didn't go back to work until they got a raise and a promise that the post office would be better run. This wildcat strike led to the Public Service Staff Relations Act of 1967, which gave union rights to most government employees. Now, more than half the union members in Canada are in public service unions.

CARPENTERS HAMMER BOSSES

Canada's first slow-down was in 1671. Carpenters came from France to start a shipbuilding industry in Quebec. Their wages had been agreed upon but it cost more to live than they had expected. They asked for a raise. The bosses said no. So the carpenters — no doubt with chips on their shoulders — staged a slow-down, taking five minutes to drive a nail and two days to saw a log. The bosses surrendered.

66

THE FIRST BOYCOTT

In 1880, Captain Charles Boycott was a farm manager in Ireland, looking after property belonging to an English earl. Harvests had been poor for several years, but he wouldn't reduce the farmers' rents and he threatened to take their farms away from them. Everybody stopped talking to him, his servants walked out, and nobody would sell him any food. His life got so miserable he went back to England. But his name stayed and became a word.

The boycott

The boycott is an organized effort to persuade people to stop buying certain goods or services. To spread its message, the boycott uses advertisements, petitions, bumper stickers, and information pickets — people who carry signs in front of a store or factory. During the 1984–1985 Eaton's strike, all union members and the public were asked not to shop at any Eaton's stores. During the VISA strike at the Canadian Imperial Bank of Commerce, union members withdrew all their money and closed their accounts at all the bank's branches.

A boycott more than fifteen years old and still going is that organized by the United Farmworkers against California grapes, in an effort to help low-paid, badly treated migrant workers employed by California fruit producers.

Sometimes an entire country is boycotted. Many people won't visit or buy products from South Africa because of its policy of racial separation, *apartheid*. In 1986, postal, telephone, and airline workers were asked by their unions not to accept any communications from South Africa. And thousands of Canadians have boycotted companies and institutions that invest money in South Africa. This is called a secondary boycott.

The general strike

A general strike occurs when all or most of the workers in a city or province or country go on strike at the same time. It's usually the result of widespread anger about a major problem like unemployment or high prices. A general strike is more than a strike: it is a challenge to the whole system. In Europe, where most workers are in unions, this ultimate weapon is common and successful. In Canada, it's rare — and rarely successful. Of the very few in our history, the most important was the Winnipeg General Strike.

THE DAY WINNIPEG STOPPED

On May 15, 1919, Winnipeg stopped working. It was the first day of the Winnipeg General Strike, the climax of many years of workers' frustration and anger. First the metal workers walked out; their bosses had refused to give them a raise, a nine-hour day, and union recognition. Then the firemen, postal workers, and telephone operators struck. They were joined by office clerks, railway workers, streetcar drivers and conductors, delivery people and garbage collectors. In all but two of the ninety-six unions in Winnipeg, every member walked off the job. Thousands of World War I veterans demonstrated in support of the strikers. Tens of thousands of workers in British Columbia, Alberta, Ontario, and the Atlantic provinces staged sympathy strikes. Even the Winnipeg policemen publicly supported the strikers. All 240, including the chief, were fired, and a special force of two thousand untrained anti-strike constables took over.

Late on the night of June 6, the federal Cabinet rammed through a change in the Immigration Act permitting the arrest and deportation of "enemy aliens." On June 18, six British-born strike leaders and a few strikers born in other European countries (who were later deported) were arrested and taken to Stony Mountain penitentiary. The workers and many thousands of non-

WINNIPEG RIOT

JUNE 101

union people who supported them were outraged, and held a parade and rally the following Saturday, June 21. On that day, "Bloody Saturday," the Winnipeg General Strike exploded in riots, violence, and death. A troop of Mounties galloped again and again into the crowd, firing their guns. The special constables, swinging baseball bats, came behind them, forcing the workers into the back streets. By nightfall, one person was dead, one was dying, and more than a hundred were injured.

In one way, the Winnipeg General Strike failed. The workers had gained nothing and lost much, including, in many cases, their jobs. Winnipeg unions were nearly destroyed. But in another way, the strike succeeded. In the years that followed many of the strikers' demands became law, and many of the strike leaders were elected to the provincial and federal governments. One of those leaders was J.S. Woodsworth. In 1933 he founded a new political party, the CCF — the Co-operative Commonwealth Federation. The CCF was sympathetic to workers, farmers, and the poor; it later became the New Democratic Party (NDP). And in 1969, fifty years after the Winnipeg General Strike, Manitoba elected an NDP government. The workers had won at last.

LONGEST STRIKE

According to The Guinness Book of World Records, the longest strike — of barbers' assistants in Copenhagen — lasted for thirty-three years, from 1928 to 1961. But Canada may have broken that record. A printers' strike begun on March 1, 1934, by Local 133 of the International Typographical Union (ITU) against two London newspapers hasn't legally ended. The ITU rules say that a local must declare a strike over, and Local 133 never did.

After wage cuts in 1932 and 1933, the printers asked for a signed contract from the Advertiser and the Free Press guaranteeing that wages wouldn't be cut in 1934. The newspapers refused; sixty printers struck, and a long stand-off began. Strike-breakers were brought in from other cities, and the papers kept publishing. Strike pay stopped in 1935 and many members of Local 133 found other jobs. Finally, in 1976, forty-two years after the strike started and with only ten members left, Local 133 gave up its charter and disbanded. But for the few survivors, the long strike against the London newspapers isn't over yet.

STRIKE WITHIN A STRIKE

In 1936, during the London newspaper strike, the Free Press delivery boys had a strike of their own. The bosses told the boys they'd have to pay eleven cents per paper per week, rather than ten cents. The boys didn't have a union, but they fought back: they scattered newspapers all over the streets and set them on fire; they overturned trucks and took them apart; and they didn't deliver any papers. After two days the Free Press gave in.

STRIKE-BREAKERS ON STRIKE

In 1957, workers at Griscom Publications, a newspaper company in New York, went on strike. The company hired strike-breakers from out of town, and got them rooms at a hotel. Two weeks later, the company said it wouldn't pay for their rooms or meals any more, so the strike-breakers struck.

NO PIZZA, NO PIZZICATO

The earliest recorded strike took place in Rome in 309 B.C., when an orchestra leader, unhappy with the length of meal breaks, walked off the job.

70

BIGGEST STRIKE

The biggest strike in Canada was the Quebec General Strike, in April and May of 1972. Almost three hundred thousand workers took part. Thirteen hospital union officers and three important Quebec labour leaders — Yvon Charbonneau, Louis Laberge, and Marcel Pépin — received jail terms and fines.

WOMEN ON STRIKE

To celebrate International Women's Year in 1975, all the women of Iceland staged a twenty-four-hour strike. The country screeched to a halt. Ten years later, on October 24, 1985, they did it again: seventy thousand women — a third of the population — stopped working for a day. And this time the president of Iceland joined them. Her name is Vigdis Finnbogadottir.

A GRAVE SITUATION

Montreal cemetery workers dug in for a long strike in the spring of 1986. They refused to bury the hatchet or anything else, including six hundred coffins stacked up in cold storage.

SMALLEST STRIKE

The smallest strike in Canada was waged by a North York, Ontario, woman in 1984. She picketed her own house until her husband and children agreed to help with the chores.

KIDS ON STRIKE

On May 1, 1986, a million black children in South Africa stayed home from school, in support of a general strike of four million black workers.

Car Wars I
General Motors Strike, Oshawa, 1937

On April 8, 1937, four thousand workers at the General Motors plant in Oshawa went on strike. They wanted eight-hour shifts, better pay, recognition of their union, and vending machines for chocolate bars. Ontario Premier Mitchell Hepburn, a Liberal, got into the act, calling the union "foreign and Communist." When Prime Minister Mackenzie King refused to send the army and Oshawa's mayor wouldn't let the Mounties in, Hepburn set up his own police force — mostly University of Toronto students who got $25 a week — to break the strike. The workers promptly called them "sons-of-Mitches." Ontario Labour Minister David Croll, appointed two years earlier by Hepburn, quit his job, saying, "My place is marching with the workers rather than riding with General Motors."

On April 23, the two sides reached agreement and the strike was over. The workers got everything they wanted except the chocolate-bar machine. The union, Local 222 of the United Automobile Workers, was recognized by General Motors as the lawful representative of the workers. This opened the way to unions in all the big industries, like mining, steel, wood, and textiles: hundreds of thousands of semi-skilled and unskilled workers were soon organized. A side effect was the damage to the Ontario Liberal Party, which many voters saw as anti-labour. The Liberals lost the election in 1945, and didn't win another until 1985.

Car Wars II
Ford Motor Company Strike, Windsor, 1945

On September 12, 1945, eleven thousand workers, members of UAW Local 200, walked out. They wanted all Ford workers to join the union within a month of being hired (a union shop), and they wanted all the workers to pay union dues. When Ford brought in strike-breakers, the workers set up an unusual picket line: they blockaded the plant with cars, trucks, and buses.

The strike dragged on and on, and, with strike pay of only $15 per week, many families were hungry. The Mayor of Windsor, who sided with the strikers, arranged that they get a little money from the city for the first few weeks, but it was soon cut off. Finally the company and the union agreed to let Justice Ivan C. Rand settle the argument, and six days before Christmas the strike was over.

Justice Rand announced his decision on January 29, 1946. He didn't give the workers the union shop, but he did say that, since all employees benefit from the union, all must pay union dues, even if they don't belong to the union. This is known as the Rand Formula, and it spread quickly to other unions and companies. For the first time, unions didn't have to worry too much about money. The strike changed Canadian labour relations forever.

The story of the MOCO strike is told in One Proud Summer, by Marsha Hewitt and Claire Mackay. Here is an excerpt about the August 13 riot, seen through the eyes of thirteen-year-old cotton worker Lucie Laplante. The strikers are in front of the mill manager's home, and Lucie's friend Jacques has a pocketful of stones:

They stood, masses of them, men and women, girls and boys, on the sidewalk in front of the big white house with the green roof. The manager's house... "No more scabs! No more scabs! No more scabs!" [they shouted].... "Shut the mill! Shut the mill! Shut the mill!".... Lucie's ears throbbed in rhythm.... Jacques drew back an arm and threw. Lucie heard glass breaking. The greenhouse, she thought. It's a goner. She grinned.

Sticks and bricks
MOCO Strike, Valleyfield, Quebec, 1946

In 1946, three thousand workers, many of them boys and girls, struck the huge Montreal Cottons (MOCO) mill in Valleyfield. They wanted an end to favouritism, bullying foremen, low wages, and terrible working conditions. They also wanted their own union, Local 100 of the United Textile Workers. The strike lasted for a hundred days, and was marked by arrests of children, clubbings, and tear-gas attacks. A riot broke out on August 13. Workers, with branches and bricks as protection against guns, swarmed through town, smashing windows and cars. Against the strikers were the Catholic Church, the Quebec government and its anti-strike squad of special police, and Valleyfield's rich people. The workers held out and the strike was won.

The victory at Valleyfield was the first step towards ending church control of Quebec unions. It showed other Quebec workers that the anti-union government of Maurice Duplessis and the powerful English factory owners could be defied and defeated. Other strikes followed, including the violent Asbestos Strike of 1949. Unions grew stronger, laws got better, and gradually, through the 1960s and 1970s, the new Quebec emerged.

Front page challenge
The Newspaper Strike, Toronto, 1964

Local 91 of the International Typographical Union went on strike against three Toronto newspapers (the *Daily Star*, the *Globe and Mail*, and the *Telegram*) in the summer of 1964. The big issue was "technological change": the newspapers wanted to use modern typesetting and printing machines, which would mean they'd need fewer workers. On orders from union headquarters in Denver, Colorado, the Toronto printers walked out. One labour writer has called this dispute "a damn-fool strike." It was certainly not winnable.

Daily Star printers on picket line.

The newspaper owners put the new machines in anyway, and hired strike-breakers to run them. When the strikers wanted to go back to work in 1965, the owners locked them out. By the time the strike and lock-out were officially over eight years later, in 1972, the printers had lost their savings and their jobs, in some cases forever.

The newspaper strike is a sad example of how new machines and processes can eliminate jobs and make old skills unwanted, and how useless it is to wage a strike against better and faster ways of doing work. Partly because of this strike, many contracts now guarantee retraining and other help to workers who might lose their jobs. With robots and computers now moving into the work place in large numbers, unions regard technological change as an important problem.

Breaking the bank
The VISA Strike, Toronto, 1985

In June 1985, the biggest bank strike in Canadian history began, when 160 employees of the Canadian Imperial Bank of Commerce VISA Centre walked out. All were members of the tiny new Union of Bank Employees (UBE) and they were taking on the third-largest bank in Canada, a financial giant worth $72 billion. The strikers were off the job for six and a half months.

"Is that trash or VISA?" Bank littered with deposit slips during VISA strike.

The Canadian Labour Congress saw this strike as so important that they gave the VISA workers strike pay of a whopping $300 a week, equal to their full salary. In February 1986, the Canada Labour Relations Board decided that both the bank and the union had to accept a contract, and scolded the bank for being arrogant and unreasonable.

The little UBE had scored a major victory, winning pay raises, a seniority clause, and protection against losing their jobs. But far more important was the fact that a union had at last gained a foothold in the anti-union banks. The way was now open to organize the 100,000 workers, most of them women, in Canada's money industry.

Public service strikes

So far, the strikes we've looked at in this section are private sector strikes: they're waged by the workers of private companies or businesses. They may be short or long, big or small, peaceful or violent. But most of them don't affect anyone other than the people involved. Others don't notice.

Strikes in the public sector are much different: they're waged by the workers who provide services to the public — you and me and everybody else. And when these public service workers — teachers, bus drivers, letter carriers, garbage collectors — go on strike, it affects everybody. Right away. There's no school. There's no bus. There's no mail. But there's lots of garbage. You notice. Everybody notices. Especially the garbage.

And because everybody notices, because everybody's daily life is upset by public service strikes, some people think they should be banned. People say these workers are too important to the community or the country to go on strike.

Unions say that if public employees are so important, why don't we pay them more and treat them better? They say that these workers strike for the same reason other workers strike: they aren't happy with their pay and their working conditions. They say that if strikes of public workers are made illegal, the result would simply be illegal strikes. And finally they say that the right to strike is a basic right of all workers in a democracy.

Some public employees, like the police (except in Nova Scotia) and the fire-fighters, have given up the right to strike. If they strike, people might die. But they do take other job actions, such as work-to-rule. And if they're deeply unhappy about their jobs, they might stage a wildcat strike, as the Montreal police did in 1969.

Other public employees have had the right to strike taken away from them. During the 1970s there were many strikes by teachers, nurses, hospital workers, and others. The public grumbled. Governments heard the grumbling and got worried. They passed laws saying some workers were essential — necessary to run the country or the province or the city — and were forbidden to strike. In the years following, more and more workers were made essential. Now, in some public service unions, nearly half the workers can't strike. And when half the workers can't strike, a strike can't work. Workers are left without a weapon.

Governments have another way of stopping a public service strike: they pass a back-to-work law. Sometimes a strike lasts only a day or two before the workers are ordered to return to their jobs. If they disobey they may get a heavy fine or a jail term. Back-to-work legislation is especially common in hospital and transportation strikes. It makes the public stop griping and it makes the government look as if it's doing something, but it doesn't solve the problems that caused the strike in the first place. They must still be settled.

Strike-breakers

Where there are strikes, there are strike-breakers: people who work for an employer whose regular employees are on strike.

Why does a person become a strike-breaker?

Sometimes it's poverty. You're out of work, out of money, and generally out of luck. You take any job you can get, even if it belongs to someone else. This happens in times of unemployment or during a depression. During a very long strike, some workers can't live on strike pay alone and may go back to work. This happened in the Eaton's strike.

Sometimes it's principle. You may be against all strikes, or against some strikes, or against a particular kind of strike. In a 1985 community college strike, some teachers continued to work, even though they belonged to the striking union.

But sometimes it's purely professional. Some people make their living by breaking strikes. They're hired by employers to spy on union members, to bring in workers to replace strikers, and even to start fights to make the union look bad.

Whatever the reason, strikers and most union people don't like strike-breakers.

ARE STRIKE-BREAKERS LAW-BREAKERS?

Quebec is the only province in Canada to outlaw all forms of strike-breaking. Companies can replace striking workers only with managers or supervisors already employed at the struck work place. British Columbia has banned professional strike-breakers; that is, employers can't hire an outside agency or service to recruit, deliver, or guard replacement workers. In all other provinces and territories, it's perfectly legal to hire people to replace those on strike. In 1986, an Alberta employer went further than that. Peter Pocklington, owner of Gainers meat-packing plant, advertised for workers _before_ a strike started. Once underway, the strike was marked by picket-line violence, hundreds of arrests, boycotts of Gainers products across Canada, public protests, and very bitter feelings, made worse because Alberta law doesn't guarantee that a striker can return to work when the strike is over. Workers can lose their jobs as soon as they walk out. The strike ended six months later on December 13, 1986, after Gainers agreed to hire back all the striking workers.

Song, to the tune of "The Worms Crawl In":

The scabs crawl in, the scabs crawl out,
They crawl in under and all about.
They crawl in early, they crawl in late,
They crawl in under the factory gate.

TWO VIEWS OF SCABS

Jack London, whose famous animal books White Fang and Call of the Wild are set in the Yukon, didn't think much of scabs. In the early 1900s, sympathetic to the poor dockworkers of San Francisco where he lived, he wrote:

After God had finished the rattlesnake, the toad, and the vampire, he had some awful stuff left with which he made a scab. A scab is a two-legged animal with a corkscrew soul, a water-logged brain, and a... backbone of jelly and glue. Where others have hearts, he carries a tumor of rotten principles.... No man has the right to scab as long as there is a pool of water to drown his carcass in, or a rope long enough to hang his body with.

An ex-steelworker, now dead, had a different way of putting it:

It was in the Depression, and jobs were scarce as hen's teeth. Me and Ruby got married anyway and by 1934 we had three kids. Couple of fellows at the plant got the rest of us organized into a union — only twenty-three of us left by then — and before anybody knew what was goin' on we hit the bricks. Went on strike, we did. Dumb trick. I said to the rest of them, I didn't want no part of it. Besides, the wife was sick, and we owed the landlord.... So I crossed that picket line they set up. I went to work every day.... But the fellows never forgave me for crossing that line. I worked right beside some of them for the next twenty years. And you know? They never spoke a word to me in all that time.

Whatever the reason, strikers, and most union people, don't like strikebreakers, and they have some ugly words to describe them:

BLACKLEG

This word first appeared in England around 1770, and it meant a thief or swindler or con artist, especially at the racetrack. Around 1850 it came to mean someone who stole the jobs of others, a strike-breaker. It disappeared from North American slang in about 1910. Why "blackleg"? Nobody is sure, but the racetrack gamblers often wore high black boots. Blackleg is also a disease of cows and sheep in which jelly-like swellings discolour the legs.

SCAB

This is a worker who crosses the picket line to do his or her own job; or any kind of strike-breaker; or a worker who refuses to join a union or to go on strike. A scab is, of course, the crust on a sore, but it comes from a word meaning "the itch," slang for scabies, an unpleasant disease caused by little bugs laying their eggs in your skin. Scabies was common in people who didn't wash too often, and by 1590, "scab" meant a "mean dirty fellow." It was first used to mean strike-breaker in 1806.

In his book *Strike!*, Walter Stewart says: "[The strike] is like taking after moths with a sledge hammer — you wind up with a lot of smashed furniture."

Many people agree. They say that strikes are destructive and wasteful, and that there must be a better way to handle labour disputes.

Part of the problem is the way industrial relations developed in North America. It's been called the "adversary system," with workers on one side and employers on the other. Each sees the other as the enemy, and their dealings with each other are conducted like a war. It doesn't have to be that way. And in several European countries — Austria, West Germany, and Sweden, for example — it isn't. Either the adversary system never existed, or it's been replaced with what's called "industrial democracy."

Under this system, workers and employers share power. They keep in mind both the good of the company they work for and the health of the country's economy. Workers don't ask, "How much money can we get out of the company?" Employers don't ask, "How little can we give the workers?" Instead, both of them ask, "How can we make our company and our country prosper?" In some years the workers may get lower wages than they might wish, but in the long run, with everyone trying to make the business prosper, the workers should prosper, too.

In industrial democracy, workers (and their unions) have much more say in how their companies and their country are run. They sit on the boards of directors of companies, helping to decide where plants should be located, how much money should be spent on machines, how fast and in what manner the work is done, and sometimes even what product is made. Workers and employers are allies, not enemies. They are on the same side, and they share the same goal: prosperity. And when people are on the same side, and share the same goal, they don't wage war — or strikes.

FINK

This is a guard hired to protect a strike-breaker; or a strike-breaker; or an informer, spy, or stool pigeon. The word was first used during the 1890s in the United States, when many companies hired men from the Pinkerton Detective Agency to break strikes and to battle strikers. "Fink" could be a rude short form of "Pinkerton."

RAT

From about 1850 on, this has meant a police spy or an informer, someone who betrays his friends, usually for money. It was soon used to mean strike-breaker, too. In England, a "rat shop" is a non-union work place.

GOON

A goon is a thug or hoodlum who had trouble passing grade three but is really good at beating people up, especially striking workers. A goon squad is a group of thugs hired to smash strikes (and strikers). The word may be partly from the old English slang word "gony," meaning simple-minded or stupid; and partly from Alice the Goon and her family, subhuman creatures in the 1930s comic strips "Thimble Theater" and "Pop-Eye the Sailor." Others think "goon" is a combination of gorilla and baboon.

Employers are better off under this system, too. Production isn't interrupted by strikes, legal or illegal. (In 1974, for example, Canada lost 9 000 000 work-days in strikes and lock-outs. Sweden lost 57 000.) Because workers help make the decisions about how fast and how hard they work and about how the company should be run, they're happier, they work better, they aren't late much, they aren't sick much, and they don't goof off. Much.

Some labour experts believe that Canada should abolish the adversary system and replace it with industrial democracy. Other people, both in unions and in management, oppose — even fear — such an idea. But as the twenty-first century approaches, something has to give.

The times are changing.

The future

By the year 2010, when your children are your age, the world will be quite a different place. Canada will change, work will change, and unions will change.

Nobody knows exactly what those changes will be, but people called "futurists" — a job, by the way, that didn't exist twenty years ago — have made some predictions based on what's happening right now. Remember that predictions aren't facts: they're good guesses.

The population of Canada will be more than thirty-two million, largely because of people coming from other countries.

The population will be older. Right now, the average age in Canada is around thirty. By 2010, the average age will be forty. There won't be as many kids your age, and there will be more people the same age as your grandparents.

Most families will have only one child, compared to four in 1960 and two in 1980. Both husband and wife will work, because two salaries will be needed.

Your children won't go to school every day. They will learn at home on computers and television sets, plugging in or tuning in to data bases and channels all over the world.

More people will have more education: half will have a college degree. And they will keep learning all their lives, sometimes for a new job, sometimes just for fun, studying old-fashioned rock music, kung fu, witchcraft, or brain surgery.

One futurist says that Canada will have millions of unemployed; another says that millions of new jobs will be created. Nobody is sure. But all agree that the trends of the 1980s, which we looked at in Section Two, will continue.

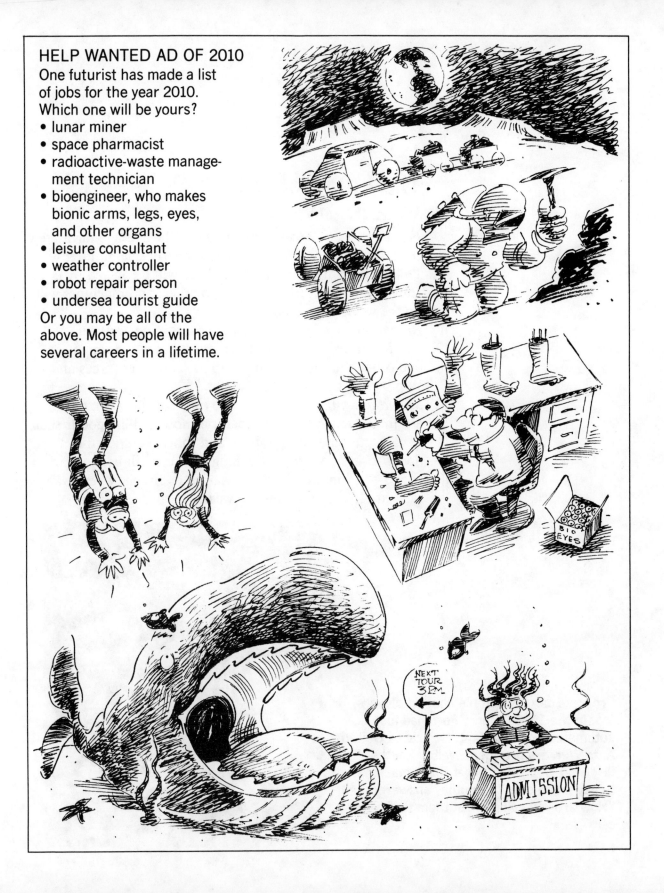

HELP WANTED AD OF 2010

One futurist has made a list of jobs for the year 2010. Which one will be yours?

- lunar miner
- space pharmacist
- radioactive-waste management technician
- bioengineer, who makes bionic arms, legs, eyes, and other organs
- leisure consultant
- weather controller
- robot repair person
- undersea tourist guide

Or you may be all of the above. Most people will have several careers in a lifetime.

The future of work

Where the jobs won't be

Farming   Farms will grow in size — the average farm grew from two hundred acres in 1940 to nearly five hundred in 1980 — but shrink in number. Many will be owned by large food companies rather than by families, and machines will do the work people once did.

Resources   In the coal, oil and gas, mining and metals, and forest-products industries, machines will do many jobs; and other countries will develop their own resources and stop buying ours.

Manufacturing   Robots will do more of the work on assembly lines; and many factories now making goods such as cars, stereos, refrigerators, and shoes will lock their doors forever. Most of the things we buy will be made in Japan or China or Korea or Mexico or Brazil, where wage rates are low and unions are weak.

Progress can be a problem for employers, too. In the 1950s, Henry Ford had just automated another plant. He said to United Auto Workers president Walter Reuther: "How are you going to get these machines to pay union dues?" Reuther answered: "How are you going to get them to buy cars?"

Where the jobs will be

The important industries — and most of the jobs — will be in what's called the service sector.

Information and communication all government services, television, computer data bases, books, newspapers, magazines, movies, plays, music, and art.

Health and personal services medicine, social work, advice (about your marriage, your children, your job, your money, and everything else), nutrition, fitness, pets, clothing, and home repair and cleaning.

Recreation sports, hobbies, travel, hotels, restaurants.

We will sell some of these services to other countries in order to buy the cars and stereos and refrigerators and shoes they produce and we don't. By the end of this century, four out of five jobs will be in the service sector.

Half those jobs will be held by women. Most women will work, and since they make up more than half the population, they may have more than half the jobs. Some thinkers call this the "feminization of the work place."

WOMEN AT WORK

Sue joined the Blacksmiths Union, and she's really forging ahead.

Liz is the boss of the bottling plant, and nothing is going to stopper.

Ann drives an eighteen-wheeler because she wants to shift for herself.

Kim is the priest in the parish, and you can't get anything pastor.

Some jobs in the service industries won't be safe from the invasion of the robots.

Chips from a chip
The science magazine OMNI forecasts that by the year 2000, North America will have nearly eight million robots. Even fast-food workers may disappear. When you take your kids to the Golden Arches, you'll be served by hamburger-making robots, and you'll order chips from a chip.

Beep... That T-shirt is no longer available. Have a nice day... Beep.
In March, 1985, a six-storey shopping complex opened in Tsukaba, Japan. It features voice-activated mobile machines that find the articles customers want to buy, and a "robot basket" that travels behind each customer to carry parcels.

Still, there's a lot to be said for working with robots. They're never in a bad mood, they don't bore you with their problems and they never ask to borrow a few bucks till payday.

NO BARK BUT LOTS OF BYTE
Some dogs may lose their jobs, too. Japanese scientists are working on a robotic seeing-eye dog that will use laser sensors to avoid bumping into things. What's more, it won't stop at a fire hydrant.

CHIP OFF THE OLD BACH

Even the creative jobs — music, writing, and art — might be in danger from high tech. A robot played the organ at Expo '85 in Japan. It said good afternoon to the audience, stared at the sheet music with its video-lens eye, memorized it in a second or two, then played it perfectly with spidery steel fingers and toes. Its eight-foot frame, heavy with cables, wheels, and gears, swayed to the music. The audience was so amazed it applauded. The robot didn't bow.

BIZARRO

By DAN PIRARO

6/5   © Chronicle Features, 1985

"Have a wonderful time on your vacation, Mr. Crosby. I'll be taking over for you while you're gone."

BACK TO THE CIRCUIT BOARD: THE TOPLESS WAITER

In 1985, an Edinburgh restaurant bought a secondhand robot to serve wine. In its first few hours on the job, it knocked over chairs and tables, broke wineglasses, and spilled several bottles of wine. Then its head fell off into a customer's lap. Both parts of it were fired.

No more nine to five

With fewer jobs available, many people will work part-time in order to spread the work around. The average work week may drop from forty hours to twenty-five or even twenty hours. And more people will decide just when they start work and when they finish, an arrangement known as flex-time.

Two people will share a job. A grade-four class may have one teacher in the morning and another in the afternoon. Or a family may decide that the father will work one year and the mother the next year. Instead of taking a few weeks' vacation, people will have long leaves of absence, up to a year, to study or to upgrade their skills.

In other words, work will no longer be the centre of your life. What you do when you're not working will be much more important, and the leisure industry will boom.

CLEOPATRA, SPY, CRUSADER; PILOT, PIRATE, OR DARTH VADER?

Did you ever want to be somebody else? Like an undercover cop, or a jockey, or a skydiver? Or maybe an alligator wrestler? By the year 2010, your wish may come true. With more leisure, people will hire the services of an "experience designer," who can make your fantasy a reality. For a day or a week or a month — and for lots of money — you could be a knight in King Arthur's court, a movie star, a baseball player, an astronaut, or anything you choose. We can see the start of this trend now, in survival games and "Murder Weekends."

Everything we know, including all the stuff in this book, can be encoded in 1,000,000,000,000,000 — that's one million billion — bits of computer information. Scientists want to send all of it into space, just in case E.T. is listening. The only problem is that it will take 37 million years to transmit.

The company picnic.

NO PLACE LIKE HOME

Some people may never go out to do anything. You'll be able to live your entire life inside your house, if that's what turns you on. Sears is now launching "video-shopping" in the United States; you can order everything from Frisbees to fresh fish on your home computer. And one futurist foresees a huge growth in what he calls "fetchits," workers who will deliver anything you want to your door.

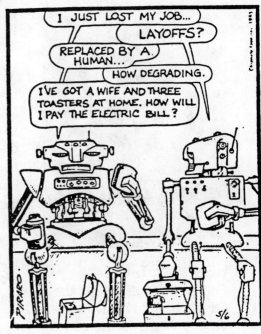

FUTURE SHOCK

Some thinkers predict a frightening future where workers will have electrodes implanted in their brains to measure activity. The more activity, the higher the pay.

THE FUTURE OF UNIONS

The workers in our mines and mills and factories — blue-collar workers — were the backbone of Canadian unionism. Now, day by day, their numbers grow fewer. Blue-collar unions are in trouble.

To get themselves out of trouble, big unions in the resource and manufacturing industries are looking beyond their boundaries for members. Workers in a library and a funeral home now belong to the United Food and Commercial Workers. Security guards in Quebec belong to the Steelworkers. Small unions are joining big unions, and weak unions are joining strong unions. Airline employees are now part of the Auto Workers, the restaurant workers merged with the Bartenders Union, and nobody will be surprised to see one big union of all the workers in the printing industry. Some observers believe that fifty years from now there will be only a few Canadian unions, each with many hundreds of thousands of members.

We've already seen that the biggest unions in Canada are the public service unions, and they're growing fast. But in the rest of the service industry it's a different story. Most workers aren't in a union. And it's to these workers Canadian unions must turn if they want to grow. The organizing of this huge white-collar work force is already underway in banks (the VISA workers) and insurance companies, department stores (Eaton's, Sears, Zeller's), and the new information industries. It will be the main target of union activity in the twenty-first century. Also ripe for organizing are the professionals, especially those who work for governments. Doctors, lawyers, architects, engineers, and even bank managers and church ministers may form unions.

HEAVY METAL
Bob White, president of the Canadian Auto Workers, has proposed a super-merger of all unions in metal working. This could mean a membership of millions, with enough clout to stop the country.

THE GLOBE AND MAIL, TUESDAY, SEPTEMBER 30, 1986   A15

Workers offer to halve jobs to postpone layoffs at GM

The Globe and Mail

Faced with massive layoffs next month, workers at a General Motors of Canada Ltd. plant in Scarborough want to work part-time to save the jobs.

Rather than lose about half the plant's 2,530 workers through layoffs that GM plans for Oct. 27, Local 303 of the Canadian Auto Workers wants all workers to work...

..."body," said Thomas McDonnell, president of the local. The "thought of the plan last Friday," days after the layoffs company announced, and pres...

While th... the un...

Ministers may form a union

EDMONTON (CP) — Ministers might form a union if the United Church continues to ignore basic justice in dealing with conflicts between ministers and congregations, says Rev. Kaye McKibbon.

Many white-collar workers who never wanted to join a union before are finding that a union contract might stop a computer from stealing their jobs. Unions now put job security at the top of their bargaining list, followed by protection against "technological unemployment." A few contracts guarantee that you won't lose your job; some give you up to three years' work at another job at your old salary; others provide for retraining or learning a new trade. But so far only one contract in five contains such protection, and unions are pushing hard for a "tech-change" clause in every agreement they sign.

For two hundred years, Canadian unions have campaigned for shorter hours. The work day shrank from twelve to ten to nine to eight hours. As new work patterns emerge — flex-time, work sharing — it will shrink further. And for some it may shrink till it's gone. To prevent this, many unions want to limit or abolish overtime, so that more people will have jobs. Part-time workers, in the past often ignored or distrusted by unions, are now welcomed. After all, the part-timers may soon be all of us.

Faced with the high-tech revolution and the threat of low wages and low-priced goods from Asia, unions and employers are looking for ways to get along, to co-operate instead of fight. The annual Canadian Steel Trade Conference brings together industry and union leaders, not to argue or to bargain, but to plan ways to keep the steel industry productive and prosperous. No insults are hurled, no fists are clenched. The time may come when such meetings are commonplace, when strikes are rare, and when industrial democracy is a reality.

Telecommuting — working at home on a computer — poses a real threat to unions, and perhaps to the telecommuters themselves. The telecommuter's home, what one writer calls an "electronic cottage," may not be much dif-

THE MIGHTY MICROCHIP

The computer has revolutionized work. It has changed our lives as much as the wheel did, and it hasn't stopped yet.

Computers will move into the work place, and humans will move out — two million of them by 1990.

Computers will move the work place right into your home. Millions of workers will become "telecommuters," linked to their head offices by computer.

Computers will move the boss right into your lap. They can easily keep track of everything a worker does, from a sneeze to a snooze to a snack, so employers are programming them to do so.

ferent from the nineteenth-century sweat shop. Banks, insurance companies, and travel agencies have already set up work-at-home systems. Most of the workers are women, and most of the work is boring. Pay is tied to how many keys you punch: the modern version of piece work. And trying to organize the telecommuters may be impossible. How can you organize people who work at home all by themselves? How can you call a strike? Where would you put the picket line?

Electronic spies are everywhere, and workers are angry. Postal unions now have a clause that allows monitoring only of groups of workers, rather than single employees. Other unions are pressing for the same thing. And the labour movement as a whole is demanding that the government pass laws to ban or limit this Big Brother approach.

They aren't alone. Many Canadians see this as part of a larger problem of invasion of privacy and the limiting of the rights of the citizen in a democratic society. Politicians, human rights activists, lawyers, and others have joined with unions to voice their concern.

Such alliances are not new. Unions in Canada have always taken a great interest in social and political issues. But in the future that interest will broaden and deepen. In a conference called "Dialogue '86," organized labour forged closer links with the women's movement, human rights groups, community organizations, the unemployed, environmentalists, peace activists, and church agencies. Together, they may change Canada.

THE LAST PAGE

The union has played an important role in the making of Canada. Without unions, we would still be working long hours for low pay, with no protection against losing our jobs, or getting hurt, or sick, or old. Unions have given Canadian workers, which is most of us, a voice in the work place and some power to shape our lives.

Chances are that one day you, no matter what your job in the Canada of tomorrow, will belong to a union. It may not be the kind of union your father or grandmother or great-grandfather belonged to. It may be ACE, the Alliance of Cosmic Explorers. Or UFAT, the Union of Fitness and Athletics Trainers. Or perhaps you will organize CAMPS, the Computer Artists, Musicians, and Performers Society. But it will be a union.

The times will change, and change again. But some things never change. Most people will always be workers. Most workers will always work for somebody else. And most workers will always need a union.

What Happened When

1497-8	1501	1534-42	1607-11	1609	1610	1629	1732
John Cabot explores the east coasts of Nova Scotia and Newfoundland and finds billions of codfish. Henry VII, pleased but stingy, gives him $50.	Portuguese explorer Gaspar Corte-Real steals fifty-seven native men and women from Labrador. He says, "They are extremely well fitted for hard labour" and sells them as slaves.	Jacques Cartier makes three voyages, charts the St. Lawrence River, captures three Iroquois and takes them to Paris, builds a fort near Quebec and goes home to St-Malo with a bagful of worthless minerals he mistook for gold and diamonds.	Henry Hudson, looking for a passage to the East, discovers the river and bay named after him; his crew mutinies and sets him adrift, with his son and seven sailors, in a small open boat. It's goodbye Henry, hello money: the bay is a fast and easy way into beaver country. Sixty years later, the Hudson's Bay Company — the oldest company in the English-speaking world — gets a monopoly on beaver pelts in all land crossed by rivers that flow into Hudson Bay.	Samuel de Champlain, map maker, patriot, explorer, the "Father of New France," learns to paddle his own canoe, and the fur trade is launched.	Étienne Brûlé, the original coureur de bois, and the first European to see Lakes Ontario, Huron, and Superior, goes to live with the Hurons. Twenty-three years later they disagree and everybody gets hot under the collar, especially Étienne; some say he is boiled and eaten.	The first black slave, a boy from Africa named Oliver LeJeune by his owner, is sold at Quebec. Although slavery is never widespread in Canada, it's 1834 before the last slave is free.	Opening of St-Maurice Forges, near Trois-Rivières, the largest and most advanced ironworks in Canada for the next 150 years. In busy periods — when it was making guns for the Americans in the Revolution of 1776, for example — the forge employed 800 men. It created Canada's first "company town."

1757-63	1812	1816	1827-33	1837	1843	1848	1853
The Seven Years' War, the first global war, with nine European countries squabbling over territory. The English and French fight for North America. The English win.	The first dock-workers' unions appear in St. John and Halifax.

The British war with Napoleon infects North America. Canada and the United States fight several battles. In 1814, thanks to the loyalty of the French and Indians and the stupidity of American generals, Canada wins. The forty-ninth parallel becomes our boundary right to the Rockies. | Nova Scotia passes a law prohibiting workers from getting together to ask for better wages and hours and sends them to jail for three months if they do. | Printers, carpenters, ship-wrights, shoe-workers and tailors form unions in Quebec and Montreal. | Rebellions in Upper and Lower Canada for more independence from Britain are crushed. Many people are executed or deported. Britain loosens up a little. | Lachine Canal strike. Labourers want more than sixty cents a day, and they don't want "store money" — a piece of paper that entitles them to supplies at an employer-owned store. A riot starts, and the army is sent to stop it. A FIRST. | The Master and Servant Act is passed, forcing servants to stay with their masters, no matter how they are treated, for a stated number of years. Captured runaways are jailed.

Shoe-makers and tailors in Montreal are afraid they might lose their jobs because of a new invention, the treadle sewing machine. They march through the streets and into the factories to smash the machines, but they are stopped by the police. | Abraham Gesner, Nova Scotia geologist and inventor, perfects kerosene. The petroleum industry begins. |

What Happened When

1855	1867	1869	1872	1873	1874	1876	1880-82
Timothy Eaton opens his first store. It's in a log hut in Kirkton, a small town northwest of Toronto.	Canada is born as an independent nation.	Timothy Eaton opens his first store in Toronto, at the corner of Yonge and Queen streets. It's 7.3 m (24 feet) wide and three storeys high.	Toronto printers go on strike for a fifty-four hour week and ten dollars a week in wages. They lose.	A fire and an explosion in a coal mine in Westville, Nova Scotia, kills sixty miners.	Daniel O'Donoghue, an Irish-born printer and the president of the Ottawa Trades Council, becomes the first labour leader to be elected to a provincial legislature.	Alexander Graham Bell invents the telephone in Brantford, Ontario.	Of the 17,000 labourers brought from China to build the Canadian Pacific Railway through the Rockies, 4000 die.

1872 (continued):

The Trades Union Act is passed, which makes it legal for workers to organize. But they have little real protection. The Act doesn't stop employers from firing workers who belong or not hiring those who might belong to a union. Employers circulated lists of workers sympathetic to unions, and those on the lists never got jobs.

1884	1885	1886	1891	1892	1894	1900	1902

1884

The Ontario Factory Act, which limits hours of work for women and children, is passed. But it doesn't apply to places with fewer than twenty workers, there are too few inspectors to enforce it, and the maximum fine of $500 means that employers ignore it.

1885

On November 7, the Canadian Pacific Railway is finished. The last spike is driven into the last rail at Craigellachie, British Columbia.

On November 16, Louis Riel, founder of Manitoba and leader of the Northwest Rebellion, is hanged in Regina.

1886

In the United States, the American Federation of Labor (AFL), a group of craft unions, is founded.

In Canada, the Trades and Labour Congress (TLC), a group of craft unions, is founded.

1891

An explosion in the Springhill coal mine in Nova Scotia leaves 125 men and boys and seventeen horses dead.

1892

The Truancy and Compulsory School Attendance Act is passed in Ontario. All children younger than fourteen must attend school.

1894

Labour Day is made a national holiday. This is a 1914 Labour Day parade in Winnipeg.

▼

LABOR DAY PARADE SEPT 2 1914 WINNIPEG NO.1

1900

The federal Department of Labour is established.

A FIRST. Arthur Puttee, hard-hitting editor of the Winnipeg labour newspaper The Voice, and Alphonse Verville, a union member from Montreal, are elected to the House of Commons.

The Great Quebec Shoe-makers' Lock-out. (see box)

1902

The Trades and Labour Congress convention votes to expel the Knights of Labor and other rival unions.

THE GREAT QUEBEC SHOEMAKERS LOCK-OUT OF 1900

Trouble between Quebec shoemakers and their employers had simmered for some time, and it boiled over when several workers were fired and replaced by foremen or non-union workers. The union went on strike.

On October 27, 1900, the employers locked the doors of twenty-one factories; 4000 people, including 205 boys and 110 girls, were out of work. The employers' association said they wanted to run the factories and choose their workers without interference.

On November 14, the employers said they would reopen the factories if every worker signed a legal document stating that he or she didn't belong to a union and didn't intend to join one, and that if any worker had a complaint, the employers' association would settle it. The answer from the unions, of course, was no. It seemed to them that the employer had all the power and the workers none. They thought it unfair, insulting, and absurd that an employers' association was trying to prohibit a workers' association.

On November 24, the owners asked Archbishop Bégin to settle the dispute, and the shoemakers agreed to accept his decision. In January 1901, the Archbishop announced his judgement. It removed the right to strike, gave employers permission to hire and fire whom they pleased, and said that the church must be involved in all union matters.

The "outsiders" — unions without a church connection — disappeared. Quebec was cut off from the rest of the Canadian union movement for forty years.

97

What Happened When

1907		1912	1914	1918	1919	1922-25	1927

1907

William Lyon Mackenzie King creates the Industrial Disputes Investigation Act, in response to an eleven-month coal strike by Alberta miners. The Act said that workers vital to the public welfare couldn't strike until a government investigator tried to solve the conflict. King is made Canada's first Minister of Labour the following year.

Collapse of the Quebec Bridge during construction because of a mistake in the design. Seventy-five workers die, including thirty-five "high-steel"

men from the Caughnawaga Reserve. In 1916 the bridge fell down again, killing thirteen workers.

The 1907 collapse is the worst bridge accident on record in the world. The mistake was a misplaced decimal point that reduced the thickness of a vertical support. After it stopped falling down, the bridge was, and still is, the longest cantilever bridge in the world: 549 m (1800 feet) between piers and 987 m (3239 feet) in total length.

1912

The Wobblies lead a strike of Chinese railway workers in British Columbia.

Beginning of a two-year strike by Vancouver Island coal miners.

1914

World War One starts.

A FIRST. Ontario passes the Workmen's Compensation Act for workers injured on the job.

Sparks from a rockfall set off dust explosions in a Hillcrest, Alberta, mine; 189 men suffocate in Canada's worst coal mine accident.

Two disasters in the seal hunt: the ship Southern Cross vanishes with 173 aboard; and Newfoundland seal hunters are left stranded on ice floes during a three-day blizzard. Sixty-nine freeze to death, eight are never found, and many of the forty-six survivors lose hands and feet.

Newfoundland writer Cassie Brown describes the tragedy in her book Death on the Ice: "Ice crusted their clothing.., even the stubble that bearded their faces; their mittens were unwieldy lumps of ice covering hands that had lost all feeling... 'Can't see,' one man muttered. Ice on his brows and lashes shuttered his eyes like blinds, and his fingers were too stiff to remove it... Many sealers...stumbled around, blind, until Jesse Collins went from one to the other, biting off lumps of ice with his teeth. He froze his lips doing it."

1918

World War One ends.

1919

Winnipeg General Strike. (see Section 4)

1922-25

Cape Breton Coal and Steel Strikes. More than once in these strikes, the coal and steel companies called in the army and hired their own special police force. They closed the company stores, turned the miners out of their homes, and cut off the water supply. Women and children were attacked with whips when they protested, and one miner was killed. Many families were close to starvation, and the union leader, J.B. McLachlan, was sent to jail.

During the strikes in Cape Breton, the miners got no help from other unions, including the AFL, with which they were linked. At that time the president of the AFL was Samuel Gompers. When he died in 1924, mine union chief J.B. McLachlan was invited to the funeral. He sent this telegram: "Sorry I can't attend the funeral but I heartily approve of the event."

1927

Old Age Pensions are introduced.

1929	1935	1937	1939	1942	1944	1945	1956

1929 — Stock market crash and beginning of the Great Depression.

1935 — On-to-Ottawa Trek of the unemployed; the Regina Riot. Faced with great numbers of jobless men, the government set up work camps — which some called "slave camps" — far away from the cities. More than 170,000 men and boys lived in them during the Dirty Thirties. They were given food, a bed, and twenty cents a day. Many joined the Relief Camp Workers Union, the driving force behind the On-to-Ottawa Trek of 1935. Led by a Wobbly named Slim Evans, a thousand men and youths rode in freight cars across the country to plead for help from Prime Minister R.B. Bennett. They started in Vancouver; they were stopped in Regina. On July 1 — Canada's birthday — during a rally at the Regina Exhibition Grounds, RCMP and city police tried to arrest the Trek leaders. A riot erupted. Downtown Regina was wrecked, more than a hundred people were hurt, and one person died.

1937 — General Motors Strike, Oshawa.

Founding of Congress of Industrial Organizations (CIO) in U.S. Beginning of unions in mass-production industries in Canada.

1939 — World War Two starts. Strikes are against the law in all industries producing goods and materials for the war.

1942 — Unemployment insurance begins.

1944 — P.C. 1003 is passed by Prime Minister King and his Cabinet (the Privy Council, hence P.C.). THE SINGLE MOST IMPORTANT LAW FOR CANADIAN WORKERS. They have the right to a union of their own choice, and employers must bargain with that union.

The Co-operative Commonwealth Federation (CCF), a political party of farmers, workers, and others wanting social change, wins the Saskatchewan election. It immediately gives its own employees the right to form a union. A FIRST.

Family allowances ("baby bonuses") begin.

1945 — World War Two ends.

The end of the war means the beginning of strikes in all major industries. In the next two years, workers win better wages, hours, and working conditions, including vacation pay. A FIRST.

1956 — The Trades and Labour Congress and the Canadian Congress of Labour merge to become the Canadian Labour Congress (CLC).

Eileen Tallman speaking to workers in 1947.

The year 1948 saw the beginning of The Eaton Drive, a four-year try at getting a union into Eaton's, and the first big push into "white-collar" territory. The drive was led by Eileen Tallman, a woman of great energy and dedication. In 1952 the long struggle was over: the union lost by a handful of votes. About the same time, more than 1000 employees of Dupuis Frères, a huge department store in Montreal, formed a union and went on strike for two months. They won. They proved it could be done.

99

What Happened When

1958

Newfoundland loggers' strike.

The Springhill Mine explosion and tunnel cave-in kills seventy-five miners. In his book Great Canadian Disasters, Frank Rasky talks about one of those miners: "Percy Rector, a fifty-five-year-old bespectacled man, died in the depths of the earth in agony because his mates didn't have a knife. Two heavy timbers had snapped shut like a giant trap on his arm. For five days, his comrades listened in numb horror to his cries. 'Please cut my arm off, boys,' he pleaded. 'O God — O merciful heavens — take my arm and let me go!'"

The Second Narrows Bridge in Vancouver collapses during construction because of faulty engineering plans. Eighteen workers die.

1959

The fishing fleet of Escuminac, New Brunswick, sinks in a storm. Thirty-five fishermen drown.

1961

The New Democratic Party is founded from the old CCF, with the support of the Canadian Labour Congress.

1963

The Canadian Union of Public Employees is formed from a merger of the National Union of Public Service Employees and the National Union of Public Employees.

1965

Postal Strike. An illegal walk-out, since public service workers weren't allowed to strike.

1966

Quebec teachers' strike. The Quebec government forces them to return to work.

Canada Pension Plan starts.

The merger of the Civil Service Association and the Civil Service Federation, to form the Public Service Alliance of Canada (PSAC).

1967

Canada's 100th birthday.

The Public Service Staff Relations Act is passed. THIS IS THE SINGLE MOST IMPORTANT LAW FOR ALL PUBLIC EMPLOYEES. The act gives them the same rights as other workers, including the right to strike (except for the Mounties and the armed forces). This law was a direct result of the illegal postal strike of 1965.

1969

The Confederation of Canadian Unions (CCU) is founded.

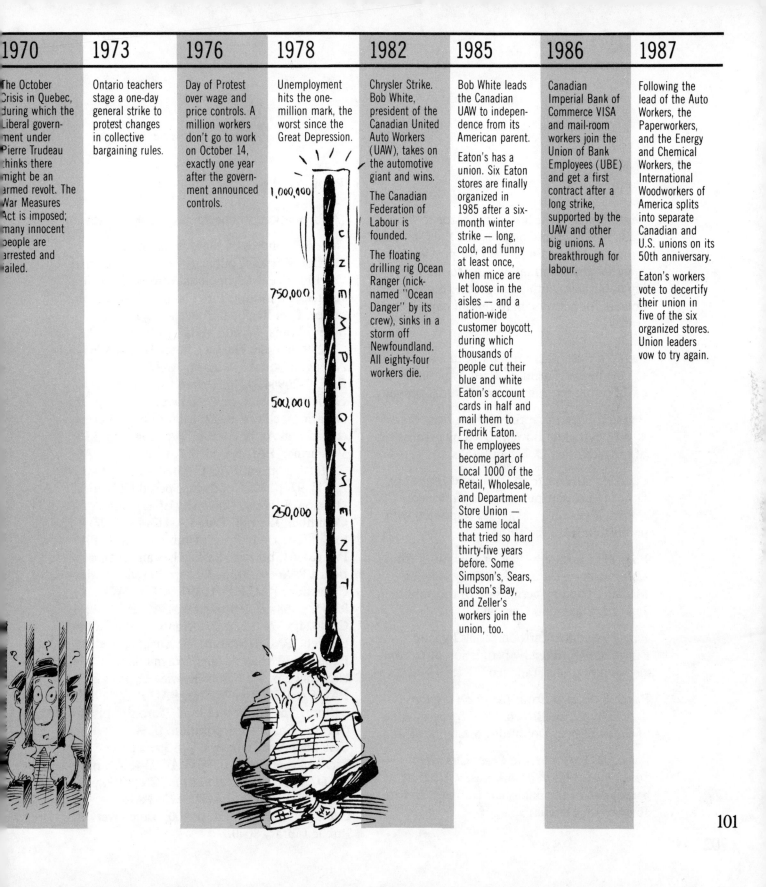

1970	1973	1976	1978	1982	1985	1986	1987

1970

The October Crisis in Quebec, during which the Liberal government under Pierre Trudeau thinks there might be an armed revolt. The War Measures Act is imposed; many innocent people are arrested and jailed.

1973

Ontario teachers stage a one-day general strike to protest changes in collective bargaining rules.

1976

Day of Protest over wage and price controls. A million workers don't go to work on October 14, exactly one year after the government announced controls.

1978

Unemployment hits the one-million mark, the worst since the Great Depression.

The Canadian Federation of Labour is founded.

The floating drilling rig Ocean Ranger (nicknamed "Ocean Danger" by its crew), sinks in a storm off Newfoundland. All eighty-four workers die.

1,000,000

750,000

500,000

250,000

UNEMPLOYMENT

1982

Chrysler Strike. Bob White, president of the Canadian United Auto Workers (UAW), takes on the automotive giant and wins.

1985

Bob White leads the Canadian UAW to independence from its American parent.

Eaton's has a union. Six Eaton stores are finally organized in 1985 after a six-month winter strike — long, cold, and funny at least once, when mice are let loose in the aisles — and a nation-wide customer boycott, during which thousands of people cut their blue and white Eaton's account cards in half and mail them to Fredrik Eaton. The employees become part of Local 1000 of the Retail, Wholesale, and Department Store Union — the same local that tried so hard thirty-five years before. Some Simpson's, Sears, Hudson's Bay, and Zeller's workers join the union, too.

1986

Canadian Imperial Bank of Commerce VISA and mail-room workers join the Union of Bank Employees (UBE) and get a first contract after a long strike, supported by the UAW and other big unions. A breakthrough for labour.

1987

Following the lead of the Auto Workers, the Paperworkers, and the Energy and Chemical Workers, the International Woodworkers of America splits into separate Canadian and U.S. unions on its 50th anniversary.

Eaton's workers vote to decertify their union in five of the six organized stores. Union leaders vow to try again.

Permissions

Grateful acknowledgement is made to the Canadian Labour Congress and the Canadian Union of Public Employees for providing material and information, and to the following publishers, authors and other copyright holders for permission to reprint copyrighted material.

Page 10: Excerpt from *Trouble at Lachine Mill* ©1983 by Bill Freeman. Used by permission of the publisher, James Lorimer and Company.

Page 13: Excerpt reprinted from *Boss Whistle* ©1982 by Lynne Bowen. Used by permission of the publisher, Oolichan Books.

Page 25: Excerpt from "Day and Night" by Dorothy Livesay, published in *Collected Poems*, Ryerson Press, 1972. Reprinted with permission from the author.

Page 86: Cartoon by Trevor Hutchings from *Computers on the Job* ©1982 by Heather Menzies. Used by permission of the publisher, James Lorimer and Company.

Page 87 and 89: Cartoon panels by Don Piraro are reprinted by permission of *Chronicle Features*, San Francisco.

Page 98: Excerpt from *Death on the Ice* ©1972 by Cassie Brown. Used by permission of the publisher, Doubleday & Company, Inc.

Page 100: Excerpt from *Great Canadian Disasters* ©1961 by Frank Rasky. Used by permission of the publisher, Harcourt Brace Jovanovich Canada.

Photo credits

[Abbreviation: Public Archives Canada (PAC)]

Page 6-7: photos of Margot Kidder and Gordon Korman, publicity photos; zookeeper Pat Eldridge, Metropolitan Toronto Zoo; fire fighter, Mississauga Fire Fighters Association; police, Peel Regional Police Association; all other photos, Wynne Millar. p. 11: top, PAC C-4239; middle, United Church of Canada Archives; bottom, Ontario Archives. p. 12: PAC C-30944. p. 14: United Church of Canada Archives. p. 17: Edward Roper. p. 21: Ontario Archives. p. 22: Library of Congress & National Archives/PAC PA-115431. p. 23: W. Farmer, PAC PA-103086. p. 25: top, PAC C-36184; bottom, PAC C-36184. p. 28: PAC PA-17197. p. 30: Goodwin, Special Collection Division, Library, University of British Columbia; Rosvall, PAC PA-117445. p. 31: top, ©The Daily Press (Timmins, Ont.), PAC PA-120663; bottom, Saskatchewan Archives Board R-A6697(2). p. 35: top, Parent-Rowley Collection, PAC PA-120397. p. 61: PAC 93715. p. 68-69: left to right, PAC C-37329; C-34024; C-26782. p. 71: Montreal Star, John Daggett, PAC-116453. p. 73: The Archives of Labor and Urban Affairs, Wayne State University. p. 74: Parent-Rowley Collection, PAC PA-118115. p. 75: top, PAC PA-93698; bottom, The Globe and Mail, Toronto. p. 84: Chrysler Canada Corporation. p. 90: Canadian Auto Workers. p. 95: Peter Rindisbacher, PAC. p. 96: PAC C-43281. p. 97: D. Millar, Myers & Co., PAC 129947. p. 98-99: left to right, PAC C3623; PAC C-24840; PAC C-98731. p. 100: Vancouver Public Library 3040.

Index

INDEX

103

PAY CHEQUES AND PICKET LINES